NEW SCARY STORIES TO READ IN THE DARK

By RJ LAWRENCE

THE WELL

Turley looked into the well but saw nothing. It seemed to descend forever to the end of the Earth maybe. He picked up a stone and chunked it in. The black space swallowed it with greed. He propped his head over the hole and waited for a clunk or a splash, but all he could hear was the same droning whir from deep within – and the voice. The soft voice that beckoned him to climb down. It wasn't soft like a lady's voice, but it *was* beautiful. It was really more like a song than a voice, he thought. A wonderful song that warmed his chest. And it knew his name. Somehow it knew his name.

"Come, Turley, come." the voice teased. "Come down inside with me."

Every day for six weeks the voice had summoned him, but Turley had never answered. And now it seemed the voice had grown frustrated.

"Turley, Turley!" it shrieked as it usually did when he turned to go home. This made the boy run and promise himself that he would never return to the old busted well in the middle of the field. But each night, while he lay in bed, he would stare out the window. And in his head, he could hear the voice pretty like music. And it made his chest feel warm.

Each morning, Turley went to school just like all the other children. But lately, his teacher noticed him gazing out the window for much of the day, while the other students did their work and passed their little notes. She didn't scold him in front of the other children. He had enough problems with bullying and taunting, and she knew it. On one particular day as the other kids were leaving, she stopped him at the door.

"Are there problems at home, Turley?" she asked. "Are you and your mother getting along alright without your father?"

He nodded but his eyes studied the floor.

"Turley, if something is wrong, you should talk to me or another adult about it. But otherwise, you need to pay attention when I am teaching class and you need to do your work with the other children."

He nodded, never breaking his gaze from the floor. She told him to go home, and he did. As the young teacher watched him leave, she lit a cigarette and imagined getting out of the small town to teach in a big city, where the schools were large and modern, and the parents didn't beat and fuck their children.

Turley had actually made it halfway home this time before the two Martin boys caught up to him. Almost immediately, they began pelting him with tiny rocks in their usual fashion. The boy knew it was better not to run, and he stopped and waited for them to catch up completely.

"Hey, Turley," Freddy, the large fat older one said as he hopped atop a large rock. "Ms. Oliver putting you in the retard class yet?"

He was only a year older than Turley, but he had already begun to develop large patches of acne on each of his sweaty red cheeks. The younger boy was named Abe and his claim to bullying was that he was Freddy's younger brother. On his own, Abe would have had difficulty bullying a large toddler, but he was known to torment many an older kid on the playground, as Freddy stood behind him, his thick arms folded, a menacing grin smeared across his face.

Abe approached Turley first and drove his fist into the boy's right arm. Turley grimaced some and then returned to staring intently at the ground.

"Man, this kid *is* retarded," Abe said to his older brother. "What should we do with him?"

Freddy's yellow smile curdled into a sneer. He hopped off the rock and strolled closer to where Turley was standing. He looked down at the lime-colored grass beneath their feet and knelt to tear off part of a crooked tree branch lying awkwardly nearby.

"I'll tell you what we should do. We should stick this branch up his stupid ass."

Abe snagged Turley's left arm, but he quickly wrenched it free from the smaller boy's grip and stumbled backward.

"Hey, kid," Abe said, his face reddened both from anger and embarrassment. "If you run, we'll stick the whole thing in sideways."

Freddy laughed at this, and then they both rushed the boy. Turley screamed and stumbled into a sprint. He rushed off the woodland trail they'd been walking on and leapt over the crumbling fence that separated the green thicket from the vast yellow fields. His awkward gate was no match for Abe's. But luckily, the boy seemed too unsure to pursue without waiting for his larger but slower accomplice.

Turley ran toward his home and then something caused him to stop entirely. A sudden rush of warmth had flushed across his chest. It wasn't the fear or the running. It was stronger and he nearly felt as though he would pass out.

"Come on!" Abe urged the wheezing Freddy on. "He stopped!"

Abe's yelling broke Turley's trance and he began running again, this time in the opposite direction of his house. He ran toward the center of the vast yellow field. As he got closer, he heard the beautiful voice call out to him.

"Tuuuurrrrley. Tuuuurrrrley." it said so sweetly.

Abe was the first to catch up to Turley, who now sat quietly on the ground by the old well. The small boy stopped several yards short to wait for his muscle to arrive.

"Hey, kid," he said. "You're in big trouble, now."

Freddy finally caught up a few minutes later. His face was bright red, and his shirt, which had already been stained by what looked like mustard, was now nearly saturated with sweat.

"Oh, man," he said in between desperate wheezes. "I'm gonna kill you."

Turley looked up at them, his fear renewed.

"I know," Abe said. "Let's throw him in the well."

Freddy grinned at this idea, and the two boys approached Turley and grabbed his arms.

"Get his legs." he said to Abe, who quickly complied.

The two hoisted Turley up and slowly carried the struggling boy toward the hole in the center of the field. Turley's screams bellowed across the plains, but there was no one within miles to hear.

As they approached the well, Abe began to wonder where things were going. Would they actually throw the kid in or just let him dangle a little? And then, he heard the voice.

"Abraham."

It wasn't soft like a lady's voice, and it was more like a song than a voice. A wonderful song that warmed his chest. And it knew his name.

"Come, Abraham, come." the voice continued. "Come down inside with me."

Both boys immediately dropped Turley and stood staring at the well, their jaws dangling as if unhinged from their skulls.

"Who the hell is that?" Freddy said with a higher pitch than was usual.

Abe remained silent.

"Come, Abraham, come." the voice said again. "Come down inside with me."

"Screw this kid and this fucking well," Freddy said. "Let's get out of here!"

But Abe said nothing. Instead, he quickly approached the well and looked down into its dark open face.

Freddy flung a panicked look at Turley, but he was only staring blankly at the ground. Then, his eyes shifted back to Abe, who had begun crawling in.

"Abe! Get down! What are you doing?"

But it was too late. The boy cleared the rocky structure around the hole and plummeted down into the pit.

Freddy stood awestruck, his mind racing between various sorts of fear. Fear of the voice that had seduced Abe into jumping into the well. Fear of his father's belt when he found out Freddy had lost his younger brother. But when the awful sigh began to pour out of the well's opening, all of his fears receded against the advance of this terrifying new one.

Turley began to cry when he heard it, and he immediately leapt to his feet and sprinted toward his home.

"Awwwwwwwwwwwwww!" the voice continued in a deeper grittier way than it had earlier. It sounded like a cry of relief, like the sound their father made after a bowel movement or the sound their older brother made when he was done having sex with the big breasted girl that lived next door. Then came the swishing noises, followed by a piercing whir. Freddie closed his eyes, pressed his hands against his ears and tumbled to the ground. The noise made him nauseated, and he felt his stomach begin to wretch out its contents. And then, in an instant, the air fell silent.

Freddy opened his eyes and slowly climbed to his feet. Tears streamed down his acne-scarred cheeks, his knees trembling as he reluctantly approached the well.

"Abe?" he called out meekly. "Abe?"

When he reached the well, he positioned one eye just far enough to see the endless circle of rich darkness that seemed to go on forever.

"Abe?" he called again, the black hole consuming his words.

He waited for some sort of reply from his younger brother, but he could hear nothing.

And then, he heard the voice and his sobs died away.

"Freeeeddddddy."

It wasn't soft like a lady's voice, and it was more like a song than a voice. A wonderful song that warmed his chest. And it knew his name.

That night, Turley's mother had to work at the hospital. She had been working most of the time since his father had run off. The folks in town felt a great pity for the two of them. But in truth, it had been the best thing that could have happened. After all, the only time his father wasn't beating her was when he was beating him. Unfortunately, now the boy's mother worked nearly all the time to make ends meet, and Turley and the television had gotten close.

Before she left, Turley's mother told him she didn't know how long she would be gone and instructed him to stay inside and watch television. It turned out some of the hospital's staff would be participating in the search for two of the Martin boys who had gone missing, and she was going to have to cover their shifts.

"Dinner's in the oven, Turley," she said, as she gathered her things and stuck her foot halfway out the door. "Make sure you brush your teeth and don't answer the door unless the neighbors come to check on you."

She kissed his head and departed for work. Turley watched her car pull out of the drive and disappear over the gravel hill. When she was gone, he shot a glance in the direction of the well. It was dusk and the sky was afire with large plumes of orange clouds. He went inside and closed the door.

For most of the night, he sat perched on his knees a few feet from the television, his brain trying to ignore the howling wind outside. His poor mind was having its way with him, distorting every swell of wind into the voice from the well.

Hours passed, and his eyelids began to take on weight. But just as he decided to go to bed, his chest began to warm. A terrible fear overtook his body, as he listened to the aching call from outside.

He sat and stared at the window curtains without moving, the voice outside sounding more desperate than before. It didn't sound like music anymore; it sounded like a hungry cry.

"Tuurrrrleey! . . . Tuuuuuurrrleeeeeyy!" it shrieked.

He climbed to his feet, repressing his urge to urinate. He moved toward the white curtains that gently danced in the simmering breeze. He pulled them a little to the side and peered out into the yard. Just at the furthest edge, where the porch light faded to nothing, he saw an extremely dark figure, its body inexplicably shaped. Similar to a man's, but freakishly put together, it seemed to be only a few inches wide at the abdomen and several feet across at the shoulders.

When the thing saw that Turley had come to the window, it stepped into the light to reveal itself. But, despite this, Turley could see little difference in its appearance. Completely black from top to bottom, the figure had an ovular head and extremely long, thin arms, legs and fingers. Besides this, it had no perceivable features at all, and resembled nothing more than a solid three-dimensional shadow.

Turley watched as the thing fully emerged from the edge of the light. It crouched down low and seemed to tilt its head as it looked at him. Tears streamed down Turley's face as the creature bawled out his name again.

The boy's sobbing became audible, and when the creature heard him crying, it collapsed to all fours and plunged its long arms forward into the ground, curling its legs beneath it like some kind of terrible alien gorilla. Quickly it encroached upon the front door of the house. Turley screamed as he heard the locked doorknob rattle.

Quickly, he ran down the hallway and into his mother's room, where he shut the door. He slowly backed away and sat quietly on the floor. As he stared at the closed passage, he heard the front door of the house concede its struggle.

Soon, he could hear the sound of ticking as the strange creature hurried down the hallway, its long, odd feet tapping against the wood floor.

Turley's mind spun, and instead of escaping through the window, he allowed his childish instincts to coerce him into his mother's closet. He climbed into it and reached up to pull down his mother's clothing from the hangers. The garments fell upon him one after another, burying his head.

As he sobbed, his mind drifted back to the day he found the well. He thought about how old it had looked and about the dull-looking dime he had tossed into it. And he thought about the wish he had made and how he had been disappointed later that night when no one had come to take his father away.

He thought about his mother and how long it had taken her to finally begin to smile; how long it had taken for her to finally allow herself to believe that the man she wished she hadn't married really wouldn't be coming back. And with the horrible creature bearing down on him this time instead of his father, he wondered if he would have done anything different if given the chance.

Turley heard his mother's door swing open with great force and within seconds the closet door was open too. The boy immediately felt the thing pick the clothing from atop his trembling body. He opened his eyes and saw its freakish silhouette eclipsing the pale orange lighting from his mother's bed lamp.

Much longer and taller than he had realized, it was only able to fit its head and arms into the closet. It shrieked and smacked as it dug through the clothing, and Turley felt its drool collecting on his arms and face.

When the creature had exposed Turley entirely, it wasted little time acting on its lust. It clasped its grotesque fingers around him and plucked him from the clothes. Its fingers nearly encircled the boy's body. And when Turley opened his eyes, he saw that it had no face at all, but only a long black head with a wide gaping hole packed full of needle-like teeth.

Turley screamed as the creature shoved his left shoulder into its slobbering mouth. His mind felt young and helpless, and as the thing fed, Turley said the only thing that came to him.

"I wish you away."

The boy closed his eyes and prayed that the going rate for wishes was two for a dime.

THE END

THE BOX

To whom it may concern:

There are those who will read this and think me either a liar or mad. It is not my objective to offer excuse for my action or, more appropriately, my inaction, or to repair the pockmark on my name. It is only my intention to record the true account of what happened between Nathan Windell and me on the night of his death. So, let the bodies believe what they may. I am weary of the mess anyway and my concern for my reputation has lost its vigor.

Nathan Windell's death was no fault of mine. Though, in truth, my cowardice contributed to it. This is a burden I cannot throw off. But I endeavor to tell the story, nonetheless.

On the night in question, he visited me at a far later hour than is generally accepted. But, at the time, I was a restless sleeper and any excuse to escape the tossing about in bed was not altogether disagreeable. I burned a candle and went to open the door. He slipped through like water, quickly and without asking. Underneath his arm he carried what appeared to be a leather box for holding shoes.

"I had to show this to you before anyone else," he said, the sweat on his forehead shimmering in the candle's glow.

I did not know why he thought I should be the first to see anything, as I did not consider him a friend and had been quite sure that his opinion of me was reciprocal. The most I knew of him was that the students at the university preferred his classes to mine; and those who know me will realize I mean this not as a compliment. He patronized his students, and I will assert that his students' futures suffered for the sake of his popularity.

His haste in entering nearly extinguished the candle I held. I cupped it with my hand until he fixed his feet. His face was flush, and he was clearly inebriated. I asked him why he had come. He misunderstood the nature of my question and told me about the box.

"It's amazing," he said. "I don't even know how to start."

He began by telling me about a soothsayer he and his fiancée, Francine, had called on, just for whimsy, I was assured. According to him, the encounter was within the ordinary of what one might expect from a sit-down with a fortune teller. That is, until the end, when the two of them settled their debt and stood to depart and attend to the rest of the day's events. The soothsayer, a very old woman with an opaque cataractous left eye, seized one of his arms and jerked him near to her.

"She looked into my eyes and told me I should go to the basement of my house and dig where the ground was moist."

Nathan said he thanked her politely, and then he and Francine continued on their way. Weeks later, he submerged into his basement in search of a pipe wrench. In the middle of the soil floor, he saw a round wet spot the size of a wagon's wheel. Though, claiming to be unbelieving, he admitted to a strong compulsion to dig - a compulsion to which he eventually succumbed. Within the wet circle, two to three feet down, he found the leather box. And now he meant to show me its contents.

I asked what it was.

"It is different every time."

To this I scoffed, which brought a wry smile to his lips.

"I knew you would feel that way. Who would believe me? I too would not as such. But we have worked together long enough for you to know that I am many things, but mad is not one of them. Agreed?"

I was considerably less sure.

"Open the box, then," I said. "Show me this miracle."

The wry smile unfurled again. He set the box on the table and raised the lid. I stooped onto the ends of my toes to look inside. Within the container, a plump caterpillar with three heads squirmed across the red felt bottom on a gooey track of mucus and scum. Nathan shut the box and opened it again. Not a trace of the caterpillar remained. Instead, a glowing ball of iridescent light hovered an inch above the bottom.

"This can't be real," I mumbled mostly to myself. Nathan opened and closed the box several more times to validate that it was.

After ten minutes of an Irish coffee break, I found vital to my nerves, we resumed the experiment. The very next oddity born from the container was no less amazing than the previous ones. And the others after that seemed even more bizarre and intense.

We marveled at each new revelation. They were things that seemed to have broken loose from another world. On one occasion, Nathan removed the lid and unveiled a flopping fish with scales that I declare were nothing more than human fingernails.

Another disclosure exposed a tiny man, no more than three inches. He seemed very agitated, spouting a language of clicks and pops. He even leapt from the box and pumped his fist at us. When Nathan closed the lid, the little man disappeared, and we began to learn of the controlling power of the box.

We proceeded for hours witnessing amazing sights that varied from hideous to wondrous. From stones that shone vivid rays of rainbow light to grotesque insect larvae with scorpion-like pinchers and the legs of spiders. The box was indeed miraculous, but after hundreds of unveilings, it took only one materialization for us to discover that it was not heaven sent.

I cannot remember which one of us opened the case the final time. I only remember the red fog that spewed into the air. Each of us covered our mouths so as not to inhale the peculiar cloud. We stood still impatiently waiting for something spectacular to happen. We were not disappointed.

After several seconds, the cloud began to contort into horrifying shapes, and Nathan cried out as the red gas settled into the form of a giant chomping skull. I stumbled backward toward the door, but the fog seemed to have no interest in me. Instead, it moved toward Nathan, backing him into the corner of the room.

"Close the box!" he yelled, but my nerves were locked. The skull's jaws slammed down loudly, and I suspected that some unimaginable magic from another world had altered the gas into something solid and deadly.

Nathan pressed his back against the wall and slid down to the floor as the hungry skull bore down on him.

"Please! Close the box!" he whaled like a child.

I tried to move my legs, but they were fastened to the floor. I grappled with my mind, begging it to release me from my fear. But I could only watch as the red cloud closed in.

Nathan stuck out his arms to stop its advance, and the skull bit down, severing them at the elbows. The limbs passed through the red gas and thudded to the floor. His mouth began to say something, probably about me closing the box. But, instead, the skull crushed his head between its smoky jaws.

His body fell limp and slid to the floor. A deep moan poured out of my mouth, and the skull appeared on the backside of the smoke. The fog began floating toward me. My legs were paralyzed, but I dove forward and dragged myself toward the table where the power sat. I reached it in time and slammed it shut. The skull disappeared and the fog vanished. Nathan's body lay broken on the floor. I began to weep.

I went that very night and hurled the box into the ocean, intending to leave the guilt and responsibility for Nathan Windell's death with it. I leave it with this account instead. I do not anticipate that it will be accepted. So be it. I wish only for the truth to be tendered before I am hanged tomorrow.

THE END

THE MANNEQUIN

The brain Allen found in his brother's closet was troubling; but the worst part was the manner in which he found it.

Their mother had phoned the night before and begged him to come over and talk to Billie. He came during the day while she was at work, and, as usual, Billie had slipped out before he arrived. Allen used his key to enter and surrendered quickly to his urge to snoop.

The first strange thing he noticed was Billie's bedroom, which had been wallpapered with newspaper classifieds. He had slathered everything with them, including the ceiling and windows.

"At least he's looking," Allen chuckled to himself.

The sight was not shocking to Allen. He had grown up with Billie, after all. He could tell some stories about his brother that would make the most outrageous eccentric shake his head in disbelief; Like when he was twelve and he painted Christmas cards for the whole family using peanut butter. Allen could still see the look on his Aunt Judy's face when the boy placed one in her hands. She didn't seem to know whether to pity the poor child or fear him.

When she was leaving, Allen overheard his aunt tell his mother that she ought to have Billie "checked out." This was a touchy subject with his mom. The truth was Billie *had* been checked out.

When Billie was nine their mother caught him painting the walls with his own feces. This combined with Billie's quiet demeanor and other odd behavioral traits had convinced both his parents that he might have some sort of brain damage. But when they took him in for all the tests, the doctors pronounced him "normal."

Not long after the tests, his mother walked by Billie's room and saw him shaving his head using his father's electric razor. She shook her head and left it alone. And that was the way it went from then on: Billie would do or say something strange, and the family would simply roll their eyes a little.

Then, one day, their father's heart finally killed him. And, shortly after, Allen went off to college. A year passed, and then another. And then, at some point along the way, Allen began getting the phone calls from his mother.

"He glued leaves to the cat," she said once. And then another time it was that he had broken both arms riding his skateboard off the roof.

Allen always calmed her.

"He's an eccentric, mom," he would tell her. "He'll probably be a writer/artist-type someday."

Allen never worried about his brother. Part of it was their extremely "normal" conversations about sports and girls. The other was the age difference. The two were seven years apart and shared very little in common. Allen's life really didn't even start until he left for college, and he hadn't spoken much to his brother since.

But he had heard all about him. His mother kept him abreast of all the strange behaviors. It had grown annoying. Her paranoia had seemed to take on weight since his father's death, and he disregarded her concerns as such. Until the night before, when she called him and told of the blood in the bathroom sink.

The newspaper classifieds were not enough to convince Allen that his mother's concerns were justified. But when he opened the closet door and saw the mannequin heads, a great coldness boiled up in his stomach.

Stacked in rows, their plastic faces filled every shelf, huge vacant eyes focusing straight ahead, like thoughtless souls trapped in some mysterious nowhere. Immediately, Allen swung around to ensure that Billie wasn't behind him.

When he was confident that he was alone, Allen resumed his inspection. He reached into the closet and lifted one of the heads: much heavier than he expected. He turned it over, so the awful blue eyes looked to the side. He noticed a large square hatch in the back of the skull. He fished around for his pocketknife and wedged the tip in one side of the hatch. It quickly popped free.

Allen removed it and held the head up to the light. He shook it around. Something peeled off the right side and plopped over to the other. It was a brain.

He immediately dropped the head and stumbled back. It took great effort for him to suppress both his urge to vomit and his impulse to scream. His guilt for not taking his mother seriously was dominated by his disgust at the rotting brain within the severed mannequin head. He stared down at the thing, its lifeless eyes gawking back up straight into his. He turned away. Part of the brain had oozed onto the dingy tan carpet.

He escaped to the hallway and entered the bathroom, turned the cold water on and splashed a sample onto his face. His mother's fears were valid. Billie was crazier than he had thought. He raised his head and stared into the mirror. He barely recognized himself. His face had grown pale, and he looked afraid. And for good reason, he thought. Equal to the horror of finding the brain was the size of it: much too large to be an animal's.

Allen threw more water onto his face. He thought about the other heads in the closet. There was at least a dozen. The thought of the police wrenching each individual mannequin head open and dumping brain after brain into sacks twisted his stomach. And then, something occurred to him that sparked even greater fears.

"The shed," he thought. "Billie's shed."

Billie's shed wasn't really a shed at all. It was a small crumbling house a few yards outside, where Billie had spent most of his childhood. The long, thin shack had been there since the first day the family had moved in, and their parents gave up early warning Billie to stay out of it. It did look dangerous, but of course, that didn't stop Billie. It became his clubhouse. Allen had only been inside once, and as far as he knew, his mother never went in at all.

You could fit a lot of mannequin heads in Billie's clubhouse, Allen thought. He lowered his head and doused his face with water one last time.

By the time Allen finally ventured outside, the clouds that had rolled in earlier I the morning were gone, and the sun was now shining brightly. The grasshoppers were alive with motion throughout the brush around Billie's clubhouse, and birds were gathering above them. Allen approached the rotted shack with care. For all he knew, Billie could be inside. Nothing about his younger brother had ever scared him before. But fear had made his footsteps heavy now. He couldn't deny that.

When he approached the heavy wooden front door, he rapped at it with his knuckles. A minute passed, but the door gave no response. Allen glanced over each of his shoulders and curled both hands around the doorknob. It wasn't locked. He jammed his shoulder into the door and twisted the dull brass knob. It squeaked loudly and gave way.

It took a few moments for Allen's eyes to adjust to the darkness. Only slivers of faint light seeped through the filthy window glass. When his pupils had expanded enough to cope, he walked inside and shut the door behind him.

Inside, everything was caked in dust. The shack was larger than he had remembered. It was thin and long and resembled nothing more than a wide hallway with a very high roof. Thick square beams stretched across the room from overhead, and on each side of him, there were large cabinets with warped wooden doors. And that was all. Billie's clubhouse was dingy but surprisingly neat.

The end of the shack was veiled in shadows. Allen's fingers fumbled against first the right side of the entryway and then the left. He found a switch and flicked it with his thumb. A single orange bulb hanging from the middle of the ceiling flickered to life. Allen's heart thumped at the orange light's revelation. At the very end of the narrow shack about 60 feet away, a fully assembled mannequin sat rigid, propped neatly on a small wooden chair.

Allen rubbed his hand against his forehead. The thing sat naked staring directly at him, its large blue eyes as vacant and penetrating as the ones in Billie's closet. Its slender legs gleamed slightly against the dim glow of the dull overhead light, and its long plastic arms lay folded neatly in its lap.

Allen reached for one of the cabinet door handles and gave it a tug. It squealed open revealing a large blunt hammer and many pairs of clear rubber gloves. He glanced toward the mannequin. It showed no interest in his activities. Allen reached into the cabinet and took out the hammer. It was surprisingly heavy. He put on his reading glasses and studied the business end. It had several scratches on it, but the metal was clean.

Allen closed his eyes and stooped his head. What had he expected to see? Blood, he supposed. You don't take brains out of people's heads without spilling some blood, after all.

He shifted the hammer into his left hand and popped open another cabinet door. He found only a box stuffed with matches and a stack of old newspapers. He shuffled through them. There was nothing of interest. He jammed the door back in place and proceeded to the next cabinet. He wrapped a couple of fingers around the handle but stopped short of opening it. This one smelled.

He released the handle and stepped back. He had been bold to this point, but now his courage began to waver. His eyes drifted to the front of the shack. Light leaked between the gaps in the door and its frame. He listened but heard nothing.

If Billie caught him, what would he do? Sure, they were brothers, but after what he had stumbled upon this day, he wasn't sure if that would save him from having his brain carved out and stuffed into the head of a department store mannequin.

Allen studied the reeking cabinet's door. The thought of their old cat running around the house with leaves glued to his back didn't seem so harmless now.

He knew he should leave; call the police; call his mother; tell her not to come home; do something and do it fast. But something drew him to the cabinet.

The voice in his head repeated its plea for him to ignore the stinking cabinet and just leave. But he could not. He was compelled to know the depths of his brother's insanity. What had Billie put in his clubhouse? Was it a big pile of rotting brains? Something worse?

Allen rubbed his hands together and took a deep breath. His left hand tightened around the hammer he had nearly forgotten about. His fingers trembled as he outstretched his right arm and slowly moved it toward the handle. He curled his fingers around it and took hold.

A sharp crack echoed through the room. He released the handle and spun toward the shack's entrance. The door remained shut as firmly as before. Another cracking noise detonated behind him, and he flipped around.

Immediately, his legs grew weak, and he stumbled backwards, eyes wide, mouth agape. The mannequin had risen to its feet.

To Allen's horror, the plastic man's body stiffened straight, and its glimmering bald head shifted on its terrifyingly thin body. Its face was frozen without emotion; but its eyes seemed alive, and when Allen looked into them, they appeared to move freely within their plastic sockets.

The mannequin lunged its right foot forward toward Allen. He took a step back to match its pace. Could this be real? Was this thing real? The mannequin raised its left foot and brought it forward.

"Get back!" Allen yelled.

As the mannequin emerged from the shadows, Allen assessed it anew. Its tall naked body bobbed ever so slightly, reminding Allen of a newborn horse balancing on its new legs. The orange light refracted against the plastic skull, except in the places where a dull-colored ooze had run out of a hatch on the very top.

Suddenly, the mannequin raced two steps forward and crouched down like an animal. Allen yelled at it again, this time waving the hammer in the air. The plastic man did not react. Its eyes remained fixed on Allen and its bobbing became more pronounced.

Allen began backing up, as if from a bear in the woods. As he retreated, the mannequin studied him carefully, its head tilted like a puzzled dog. Finally, Allen turned and moved suddenly toward the door, but this seemed to trigger something in the creature, and it quickly darted forward and stopped a few feet in front of him.

Allen raised the hammer and centered it just over the mannequin's head. His heart throbbed against his chest, as the plastic person leaned forward and studied his face. It raised one of its rigid false hands and slid it gently against his right cheek.

Allen swallowed hard as it continued exploring. Then, suddenly, it jabbed its thumb into the middle of his chin. The act brought considerable pain. But Allen didn't dare flinch for fear that he may startle the thing. And then, without reason, the mannequin froze solid and remained that way for several minutes.

Allen remained still, his mind desperately sorting his options. He waited longer and then, still longer, until the fatigue in his legs threatened to send him to the ground. He closed his eyes tightly and opened them again. The malfunctioning mannequin was as still as its department store brethren.

Allen turned his head and looked at the door. It was only a few feet away. He raised his left leg and pulled it backward. He planted it and followed with the right. A crack came from the joint in his knee, and the mannequin sprung back to life. Allen yelled and brought the hammer down hard on its head. The mannequin ignored the blow and lunged toward Allen's feet, knocking him backward.

He screamed and collapsed to the ground, as the mannequin quickly moved upon him with surprising dexterity. It crouched at his feet and gathered the top of his right ankle in its hands. Allen kicked at it, striking it repeatedly in the shoulder with his one free foot. But the mannequin's grip was like a vice. It twisted his leg in a circle, and Allen felt his knee pop under the strain of its amazing strength.

Hysterical shrieks poured from his mouth as the mannequin pried and twisted his leg completely around. He heard the bones and cartilage snap beneath his skin and felt the cap burst loose from its mount atop his knee.

The throes of pain sent Allen to the verge of passing out. The plastic creature at his feet began to seem like a dream, as he fell into the recesses of a comforting tunnel vision.

When the door flung open and light poured into the shack, his mind snapped back into place for a moment and then receded again. He was aware of very little: the smell of the damp rotted wood; the dull orange tint from the bulb dangling overhead; Billie's voice, and the mannequin cowering at the sound of it. His brother's thin, pallid face. The mannequin collapsing to its hands and knees and scurrying to the other side of the room. Darkness. Dreams. And, finally, bright light from overhead as he regained consciousness.

He tried to raise his hands to block the light, but they would not move. He looked forward through bleary eyes to see Billie standing before him, a small circular saw in one hand, a scalpel in the other.

"I'm so sorry, Allen," he said. "Bernice is one of my favorites, but she's a bit unpredictable."

Allen tried to speak, but nothing happened.

Billie looked down at the floor for a moment and then back to his brother.

"I'm afraid an artery ruptured in your leg, and there was just too much blood loss."

He set the instruments on a bloody table and took up a small mirror. He approached his brother and held it to his face.

"Forgive me. I didn't know what else to do."

Allen searched in vain for his reflection, a horrifying image in its place. He wept, but the vacant eyes in the mirror remained dry.

"Don't worry, Allen," Billie said. "We'll think of something."

And with that, he began whistling as he sealed the hatch on the back of his brother's plastic skull.

THE END

TOOTHACHE

Pauline was already awake before the alarm got to wailing. Two miserable hours of sleep was all she had been able to muster, and that was with the help of sleeping tablets. The pain in her jaw was excruciating. She groaned as she propped herself to a sitting position, her jaw throbbing angrily as the blood rushed from her head to the other parts of her body.

She was a pretty girl, although it would have been hard for anyone to notice through the grimace she had worn for the past several days. She had long blonde hair, an athletic body and a face that had retained the girlish glow of her early childhood. Right now, that face was disproportionately swollen on the left side from a furious toothache.

A long, seeping sigh powered her to her feet, and she staggered down the bright, narrow hallway that led to the bathroom. The tiny room did nothing to help her demeanor. It had been smothered in excessively flowered wallpaper when she moved in a year before, and little action had been taken to correct the mistake.

In the southeast corner there were scratch marks just above the mirror where she had tried to remove the paper. It had refused to budge, and she put it off to a more convenient day that had never come. What followed was the same useless routine of the past several days: A hot shower, salt-water and little – if any – relief.

Despite her early rise, Pauline once again found herself at odds with the clock. It was due to the usual suspects: lost keys, a run in her pantyhose and a ringing phone she had been unable to resist.

After a tactful disposal of the caller, she scoured the room for her keys before finally plunging her fingers between the cushions of her sofa. She clasped them around the handful of jagged metal, fled her apartment and ran to the elevator which she rode to the bottom floor. As usual, there were no cabs in front of her building, and she had to walk about a block before one finally swooped in to pick her up.

"Where to, lady?" the cab driver asked, and armed with her answer, he delivered her to the relatively modest office building where she worked.

She hadn't trundled forward two steps off the elevator before her boss, Samuel Martin, demanded she go to the company's dentist. She had hated dentists since childhood, never forgetting the one that had ruined it all. She was twelve, and he had a booger of a time extracting a dead tooth from her gums. She left his office in awful pain with dark bloodstains on her yellow sundress.

"Our guy is different," Sam had said. "Hell, Stanley had him put him under when he went. Said he couldn't manage his brain in a dentist's office. Apparently, he got it so bad one time, he went nuts and spit his rinsing water all over the dentist's face. Then he ran out of the guy's office and drove home with that bib thing still attached to his neck."

Pauline remained unconvinced despite Sam's assurances. It took one final demand to make her understand that this hypothetical trip to the dentist was going to become reality. She knew as well as anyone that Sam was a friend until he had to be the boss. Then he was relentless.

She gathered a few things from her office and moped back to the elevator. Sam gave her a little bit of homework and told her if she needed to drop out of the weekend's conference, he could make other arrangements. Pauline assured him she would be fine, and with that she was on her way down the elevator and into a cab pointed straight toward one of her most stubborn fears.

She entered the dentist's office expecting it to be flooded with the familiar sickening light-headed smells of nitrous oxide and various sterilizing agents. But she was shocked to discover that the room had a clean, fresh smell to it. And the walls were not the depressing white she had expected to see. They were lined with false wooded wallpaper that reminded her of the interior of the warm cabin she and a few friends had shared on a spring break ski trip years ago.

The call from the receptionist broke the spell.

"Can I help you?"

Pauline felt the sweat gather in her palms. She was tempted to answer back that she was in the wrong room, when her jaw, as if sensing a possible betrayal, unleashed a series of deep throbbing attacks.

"Pauline Selvy for Dr. Freedent," she said.

"Fill out these forms, and the doctor will be with you in a moment."

Pauline filled in the requisite fields and passed them over to the receptionist. Then, she grabbed a magazine and found a seat near the door.

She spent the next ten minutes searching the faces of the patients that emerged from behind the extraordinarily tall, shiny, red door leading to the dentist. To her delight, their faces all seemed relaxed; although, there was one girl in her mid-twenties that moaned a few times through a mouthful of cotton.

About thirty minutes passed before a fat, redheaded nurse popped her head through the eleven-foot doorway.

"Ms. Selvy?"

Pauline stood up.

"He'll see you, now."

Pauline followed the plump middle-aged woman through the shiny red door and down an uncommonly intricate maze of hallways. Finally, the nurse pressed open a door exposing a large white room that smelled very sterile.

"Go on inside and he'll be with you in a moment."

The nurse left and Pauline sat down on a tall stool just to the side of the reclined chair. She eyeballed it slowly. It was a place where countless ordeals had no doubt taken place. She shivered as she imagined the screaming ghosts of root canals and teeth being ripped from moaning mouths. She barely had time to survey the room before the door popped open again to reveal a very tall man with baseball mitts for hands.

"Hello…" Dr. Freedent glanced at his clipboard, "…Ms. Selvy." He forced the door shut behind him. "What seems to be the problem?"

He appeared to be in his mid-forties, though, he could have been in his fifties, she supposed. His hair was very dark with a few gray strands above the ears. His arms were bony and thick with hair, and his hands were quite large and thick, despite the rest of his body. They appeared to Pauline as awkward as the horrible dental instruments on the tray beside her.

"I think I have an abscess," she answered.

"Well, let's have a see."

She lay back on the reclined chair and reluctantly opened her mouth. Dr. Freedent shoved the usual dentists' utensils past her lips and began to poke around.

Pauline moaned deeply when he finally struck gold.

"Ah, yes," he said. "That's a ripe one."

The doctor laid his pointy tools on the table. They were horrifying. Some were gnarled with crooked spikes. Others were thin and seemed needlessly long.

Dr. Freedent pulled his mask down beneath his pointed chin.

"You'll need to come back later this week, so we can fix that up."

Pauline shifted to a sitting position on the chair.

"I can come Thursday," she said.

The doctor scratched his chin and looked thoughtful.

"I believe I'm booked up solid for Thursday," he said. He removed a black leather booklet from his pocket and began thumbing through it. "How about Friday?"

"I can't," Pauline shook her head. "I am leaving town early Friday morning for business."

"Well," the doctor quipped. "I'm not sure a woman in your condition should be putting work ahead of health. But since this is an obvious emergency, I suppose I could make myself available Thursday evening if you are so inclined."

His face was pointed down, but his eyes were peering up at Pauline.

Pauline's spine shivered at the idea of being at the dentist after dark. But the sooner this whole ordeal was over, the better, as far as she was concerned.

"That will be fine," she said.

"I'll make arrangements to have everything ready for you, say, about seven o'clock?"

He seemed almost eager. Like he was somehow looking forward to setting her mouth afire with pain.

"I appreciate it," she lied.

The next morning was Tuesday, and it came and left without much thought of her rendezvous with Dr. Freedent's metallic toys. But by Wednesday evening, the reality of what was in store for her began to flop and churn within her head. She didn't bother trying to gum any sort of dinner down that night. Her fear had squelched any appetite she might have had.

Sleeping pills be damned, she knew she would not sleep easily on this night. So, she stayed up and watched television with periodic, half-hearted attempts at some semblance of slumber.

When sleep finally arrived, her dreams did nothing to soften her fears. Each was splashed with subtle and not-so-subtle reminders of the day to come. In each dream, the dull taste of metallic instruments always felt fresh on her tongue, and the searing sounds of the spiraling drill seemed to haunt every scene.

One began with her swimming alone at night in a large lake in the middle of the woods. At one point she swam deep into the water until the depths began to collect all the light from the surface.

When the blackness finally doused the last bit of light and she was completely blinded, a sharp pain sliced into her lip, and at once, she felt herself being pulled to the surface.

She had this same dream at least three times, and every single instance ended with her dangling from a giant fishing rod and reel held tightly by Dr. Freedent, his face defined by an extraordinarily broad smile of satisfaction.

Though unsettling, the dreams never held the necessary thrust to wake her, but they did make for a shallow, restless night of sleep.

The next morning arrived sharply jarring Pauline conscious from the short stint of sleep she had been floundering in. She groaned as she climbed to her feet. Her mind scattered to cope with the impending fate of the day. Her brain made every attempt to rationalize a way out of it. But the pain in her mouth left her with little resolve. The agony was too real. She had to go, and it could not be put off another day.

Her work hours were difficult, and the pain pills Dr. Freedent had given her made it difficult to concentrate. Sam had given her ample opportunities to bail out of the weekend trip to Seattle, but each time she had shaken him off. The truth was, she needed this trip. It was her big break in a career that had seen male co-worker after male co-worker promoted ahead of her. The long line of disappointments had served as cruel compliments to the cold depression she had collapsed into since moving to the city from her rural hometown. There the grass had been green, and she had been prom queen. A business degree from the city's community college had set her up to leave that world for more "luminous" horizons.

Now that place seemed so distant in the sea of smog and icy shoulders, she found herself surviving in. The late nights at work, mushy TV dinners, and hollow dates with middle-aged accountants served only to push it further and further away. She was the lucky girl who made it out of that fruitless small town.

"Not lucky," her dad had always said. No, she often thought, her dad had been right. Luck had nothing to do with this.

It was dark when she arrived at Dr. Freedent's office. The receptionist had already left, and the nurse was gathering her things to go home for the day.

"There will be a medical student arriving in about thirty minutes that will be witness to the surgery," she said.

And then she went to tell the doctor that Pauline had arrived.

Pauline sat down and began to thumb through the same magazine she had read three days before, always keeping one eye on the shiny red door. It did not take long for the doctor to poke his head from behind the monstrosity.

"Hello, Pauline. How are you feeling?" he asked, though, the swell in her jaw should have been enough to answer his question.

"As well as can be expected, I guess," she mumbled as she placed the magazine down on the table in the middle of the waiting room floor.

"Well, come this way and we'll have you feeling better in no time."

Pauline rose to her feet and passed slowly through the door as Dr. Freedent held it open with the palm of his right hand. Then, they passed down the maze of corridors to the room where, day in and day out, he worked his horrific dental magic.

The weekend trip was a little difficult, but it went off without much of a hitch. Pauline felt good about her presentation, and Sam said there were bright things ahead for someone who was willing to tough out a little pain for the company. He even gave her the rest of the week off.

She arrived home on Monday and had the most complete night of sleep in quite a long while. The next morning, she awoke with an insatiable appetite, and it was clear that she was back to her old self if not better.

The appointment with the dentist turned out surprisingly well thanks mostly to the anesthetic Dr. Freedent's student had helped administer. By no means was she looking forward to her follow-up appointment the next day, but she had to admit that things were considerably better without the haze of agony she had endured over the previous several weeks.

She was greatly looking forward to a pain-free week and was just going over how she might be able to spend it when she heard the chiming of the doorbell.

Pauline walked to the door and peered through the eyehole. A large balding man in his early thirties was standing next to a stumpy-looking woman that appeared to be about the same age.

"Who is it?" Pauline asked and the man spoke.

"My name is detective Greg Wiley, Ms. Selvy." He shoved a badge up to the eyehole. "We'd like to ask you a few questions."

Pauline opened the door.

"Please, come in," she said. "Is something wrong?"

The two entered her apartment and followed her down the abbreviated entryway that led to her living room.

"Can I get you some coffee or something," Pauline asked.

"No, thank you," Detective Wiley said flatly, and the woman beside him seemed even less enthusiastic over her gesture.

There was an unusual silence for the next several seconds before Pauline finally asked again if something was wrong.

"We are gathering evidence for a criminal investigation, and we're hoping you can help us," Detective Wiley said.

Again, nothing was said for several minutes, and the strangeness of the situation began to make Pauline feel a little nervous. She was about to ask what she could do when Detective Wiley cocked his head and said something that struck her as a little odd.

"You would want to help if you could, wouldn't you, Ms. Selvy. I mean, if someone did something. -- something horrible -- you would want to help bring justice to that person if you could. Right?"

Pauline was struck by the change in his demeanor. He sounded desperate but aggressive, and Pauline got the feeling he had asked this same question many times before.

"Of course I would," she replied and, at once, Pauline was thankful she was not alone in her house with this man, detective or not.

Detective Wiley and the woman looked at each other and seemed to nod.

"What's going on?" Pauline asked with a lump in her throat.

The woman stepped in front of the detective and spoke.

"We haven't been completely honest with you, Pauline," she said. "The truth is Detective Wiley isn't here officially, and I'm not a detective at all."

Pauline took a step back.

"Pauline, my name is Teresa, and Detective Wiley is my brother-in-law."

She was short and not very fit. Her glasses were thin and sat at the tip of her nose. Her voice was calm and stable like someone talking a jumper from a ledge.

"We are here because of Bill Freedent, and we hope you'll be willing to help us."

Pauline's eyes bounced back and forth between the two strangers in her living room.

Wiley was silently kicking at the floor.

"What about Freedent?"

"He was my wife's dentist," Wiley said without looking up.

"Did something happen?" Pauline asked.

Teresa's face hardened, and she looked back at Wiley who gave some sort of permissive nod.

"She committed suicide," Teresa said.

Wiley began to kick at the floor again.

"I'm very sorry," Pauline said. "But I don't see what this has to do with --"

Teresa raised her hand to silence her.

"I realize this is going to sound crazy," she said. "You have no idea how many times we've been through this conversation. No one wants to hear this. It kind of makes people defensive and sometimes even a little crazy."

"Hear what?" Pauline snapped. She was scared and out of patience. "What are you people talking about?"

"He did something to her," Wiley blurted and then his voice softened. "While she was under."

He was staring blankly at the floor.

Pauline stiffened as Wiley's words wriggled into her ears. The blood raced out of her face as she began to think of herself sleeping helplessly under the cloud of anesthetic. Helplessly dreaming on that reclined chair while God knows what was being done to her. Sleeping behind that awful shiny, red door that led to Dr. Freedent's office.

"What do you mean, 'something'. You mean, rape?"

"I don't know." His voice was less stable now. "We don't know."

Teresa looked at him and squeezed his arm.

"The truth is, Pauline, neither of us know what he did," she said. "We just know he did something."

Pauline's eyes darted from one to the other.

"How do you know?"

Teresa began the story while Pauline steadied herself against the door that led to her little kitchen.

When she had finished, and Pauline had told them all that she could, Teresa stepped forward and reached for her hand. Pauline jerked away, and Teresa relented.

"I know this is a hard thing to ask, Pauline, but we need your help. You have to stand up and do something. If you won't help than you're just helping him do these things to others, and that makes you just as responsible."

Pauline glared at her.

"I don't know," Pauline said, and tears began to stream down her face. "Why don't we just go to the police?"

"The police won't help, Pauline," she said. "They've investigated Freedent as a favor to Greg several times and have found nothing. They say they've done all they are willing to do. Greg has pushed this so far, his lieutenant says he'll be fired if he brings the subject up again. You are our only hope."

Teresa paused and looked at the floor and then back at Pauline.

"Or, at least, until the next one."

Pauline's mouth tasted bitter, and she began to sob a little.

"I don't know what you want me to get," she said as she stared at the floor. "I have no idea what to look for."

"One of the women we spoke with worked as a nurse for him for a while," Teresa said. "She said she once found some pictures and tapes in a closet in his office. She said when she asked him about them, he screamed at her and grabbed her arm so hard that it bruised. He fired her the next day."

"What happened to her?" Pauline muttered without looking up, and at once Wiley lunged toward her, grabbed her by the arms and pinned her against the wall.

"Don't you get it?" His eyes were bloodshot and wild looking. "She's dead! She killed herself! Just like all the rest! And that's what you'll do too! We'll come back to your house next week, and you'll be dead! You'll take a knife and gash your wrists, or you'll get a gun and blow up your brains! Maybe you'll step in front of a bus or jump out of that window right there, but it is going to happen!"

His hands tightened around her arms, and he lowered his face within an inch of her own.

"It always happens."

He let go and ran out the door, leaving Pauline hysterically bawling. Teresa put her arms on her shoulders.

"I'm afraid that what he said is true," she said quietly. "We know of at least eleven of his patients that have committed suicide, and I'm sure there are several more."

She slid her fingers down Pauline's arms and closed them around her shaking hands.

"We don't know why," Teresa continued. "Maybe he's killing them and making it look like a suicide. Maybe they all remembered something terrible he did to them, and they couldn't take it. Maybe it really is all just some unimaginable coincidence. All we know is if he is responsible, he has to be stopped."

Pauline steadied herself against the wall and took in a few shallow breaths.

"Okay," she said. "I'll try."

Teresa smiled a sympathetic smile and squeezed her arm.

"I don't know how I'll do it," Pauline continued, "but I'll try."

That night, Pauline, went over it all as she lay in bed. The tragic story of Wiley's wife and her sudden unexplainable suicide tumbled around in her head like clothes in a dryer. Teresa said she had been an upbeat happy person up until the final moments of her life. Wiley had come home from work at his usual time one afternoon to find her in the upstairs bathroom with the door locked.

"Elisabeth?" he had called. "Are you alright?"

He could hear her vomiting in the toilet in between flushes.

"Elisabeth?" he called again.

She answered with a gurgling series of words he was unable to understand. Then she began to vomit some more.

"I'll get you some water," he said, and he walked downstairs to the kitchen. He had barely filled the glass halfway when he heard the shot. Apparently, she had gone into the bathroom with the .45 caliber pistol he kept in his bedside table drawer.

That was it. No explanation. No good reason. She had never spoken of suicide in her life, and their marriage was happier than it had ever been. Further confusing the issue was the fact that Teresa had just spoken to her an hour before when they had made plans to see a movie later that night. She had been cheerful, Teresa noted, and had even cracked a few jokes.

Nothing had happened to cause her to become depressed. No drastic changes in her life. No deaths of any particular loved one. Nothing to go on. Only the fact that Dr. Freedent had given her a root canal just two days before.

It all sounded iffy to Pauline. Or at least it did before they had mentioned the other suicides. She wasn't sure what to make of that. The truth was she didn't know Teresa or Wiley any better than Dr. Freedent. In the end, what made up her mind was the lack of any apparent motivation on their part to lie. Maybe they were crazy or at the minimum desperate, but she had to know for sure. She couldn't live with herself if she turned a blind eye to the possibility that she herself had been violated.

The next day, she arrived at her follow-up appointment with Dr. Freedent like a cowering dog. She stood outside for several minutes before she finally mustered the courage to make her way inside.

The receptionist recognized her and told her to have a seat. Pauline didn't bother pretending to read any of the magazines this time. She just sat staring blankly at the tall, ominous red door that seemed larger than ever.

Her hands began to tremble, and over and over she pleaded with herself to pull it together. She closed her eyes and took several deep breaths. A full hour passed and still none of the nurses had appeared to invite her back. It was as if Freedent knew of her mission and her thin commitment to it.

When one finally did appear, she was both relieved and nearly paralyzed by her fear.

"Ms. Selvy?"

Pauline struggled slowly to her feet. She felt like she had just stepped off a dizzying ride at an amusement park. Her legs were as sturdy as two giant licorice sticks as she followed the nurse through the maze of corridors. She was careful to survey the system of hallways along the way in case she had to get out of there quickly.

The nurse planted her in one of the rooms and told her to wait. Just as with her first appointment, she did not have to wait long for the door to swing open.

"Hello, Pauline," Dr. Freedent said. The grin on his long pointy face sliced through what little courage she had. "How are you feeling?"

"Better," she said, and she struggled to feign a weak smile.

He raised his mask and lowered the chair.

"Open," he ordered, and she obeyed. He began jabbing around her gums.

"Everything looks good," he said. "Everything looks very good."

Pauline's heart was throbbing out of control. Her mind was flashing with sickening thoughts of Freedent's unknown supposed perversions.

He poked around her mouth a few more times, then backed away and removed his mask. Pauline closed her mouth and sat up.

"You do have a couple of cavities, but I think they can wait," he said.

She felt his hand on her right knee.

"Just make sure to keep after them with your brush." The strange smile he had been wearing broadened. "And, of course, don't forget to floss."

Pauline nodded and swung her legs around the chair to stand. Freedent's hand slid off.

She followed him out and said goodbye, and as he walked down the hall to his next appointment she headed toward the main lobby. She was s few feet from the door, when the young nurse Teresa had told her about caught her from behind.

"Can I help you, Ma'am?" she asked.

"I left my purse here last week," Pauline said. "Dr. Freedent said I could get it from his office before I left."

"I could get in big trouble for this," she whispered back. "Do you have the money?"

Pauline nodded.

"You've got five minutes -- that's it."

Pauline followed her down the hall to a broad door labeled "Doctor William Freedent."

"I'll wait out here," The young nurse said. "If he comes, I'll ask him to come and look at something."

She unlocked the door, and Pauline handed her the four hundred dollars Teresa had provided. She then slipped in and closed the door.

There was nothing atypical about the office. There was a large classic-looking desk flanked by huge gray filing cabinets. There was a beige sofa and a small black chair directly across from an oak desk.

Immediately, she went for the closet in the right corner of the room. She twisted the knob, but it refused to turn. She hurried back to the front door and stuck her head out.

"I need the key to the closet," she whispered to the young nurse who was standing impatiently by the door.

"That's not part of the deal," she said.

"Please," Pauline begged, and she handed her another fifty dollars from her own pocket. The nurse handed her a large key ring and told her she didn't know which one it was.

"I took these keys from his coat this morning," she said. "You'll have to try them all, but hurry!"

Pauline closed the door and ran back to the closet. She jammed a silver key into the lock, and it only went in halfway. She tried the next and then the next.

"Dr. Freedent," she heard the nurse say. "Can you come look at this file up front?"

"In a second," he answered. "I have to get my schedule from my office."

Pauline's temples thumped madly as she crammed another key into the lock. She turned it, and the knob twisted free. She jumped inside and closed the door just as Freedent entered the room.

Her heart pumped wildly as she stood frozen in the blackness. She began to hyperventilate a little as she listened to him shuffling things around in the room.

After what seemed like forever, she heard the front door to the office close, and soon after, she could hear him talking to the nurse outside the door. She waited for their voices to fade down the hallway before she opened the closet door.

Her hair was drenched with sweat as she climbed out. Quickly, she began rummaging through the contents of the closet. She ripped open several cardboard boxes without finding anything but a few papers, files and an occasional box of staples or paperclips.

She was just about to give up and hurry out when she came upon a long black gym bag under the last box she had been going through. She pushed the box aside and unzipped the bag. It was full of videotapes. She picked one up in her hands and turned it over. There was a white sticker with the name Linda Hawkins written on it. She dropped it and grabbed another. It read Claire Simmons. Pauline swallowed hard. She plunged her hands into the bag and began going through them one by one as fast as she could.

She whizzed past the tapes named Barbara Stewart and Elisabeth Grant with a budding fury in her gut. Then, finally, she saw it. She picked it up in her hands and turned it over. "Pauline Selvy," the tape read. Tears began to well in her eyes as she shoved it down the front of her slacks. She opened the office door and ran down the hall without stopping to look back. Several patients gasped as she burst through the tall, red door. The receptionist called out to her as she rushed past and out of the building. She ran for several blocks in a fit of tears, before she finally hailed a taxi and made her way home.

When she arrived, she paid the taxi driver and took the elevator to her apartment. She unlocked the door and removed the tape from her pants. She studied it with teary eyes for a few moments, set it on top of her television and collapsed onto her couch.

The tape stared at her from atop the TV, and she stared back with the same blank expression.

"What was on it?" she asked herself, and then scolded her brain for trying to pretend as if it didn't know.

Her body exposed helplessly beneath that awful grin of satisfaction. His body bearing down on her slowly – those large creeping hands probing every crevice of her naked, limp self.

All at once, she collapsed beneath the brunt of her misery and began sobbing uncontrollably. She reached to the lamp table and swept up a picture of her father taken before she had moved from home and before the Alzheimer's had chewed up the last of his marbles.

"Oh, God," she whispered, and she collapsed in a fit of anguish. For a moment, she considered just sending the tape to the police. The simple fact that the tape existed was undoubtedly enough to prosecute Freedent. But what was on it? What would they see? She had to know what was done to her. Even if it killed her, she had to know.

Slowly, she gathered herself and climbed to her feet.

She took the tape in her hand and pushed it into her video player, and it immediately began to play. At first, all she saw was black and then, a weak light popped on somewhere off camera. At once, she saw herself lying motionless on the reclined chair. There was no sign of Freedent, the dental student or anyone else for that matter. She was lying alone in the middle of the room.

Pauline's sweat turned cold as she waited for something to happen. Finally, after several seconds both Freedent and the dental student came into the picture. They mumbled to each other for a few minutes all the while ignoring the unconscious woman sprawled out on the chair behind them. After what seemed like a long time, they shook hands and the dental student left. Freedent locked the door and turned to look at Pauline sleeping silently on the chair. He slowly walked toward her, his arms crossed loosely against his chest.

Pauline's hands had crept up to her face when she began watching and now, they were partially shielding her eyes. Her emotions fluttered between fear, rage and absolute despair as she tracked the dentist's every move.

His head cocked to one side, Freedent reached down and cupped the sleeping woman's jaw in his gigantic right hand. Over and over, he raised her head in a nodding motion. Then, he poked his index finger into her mouth and moved it slowly against her lips in a circular motion. After this, he raised up again and stared down at her for several minutes. Then he stepped back and began pacing around her over and over, his hands clasped behind his back.

Pauline's mind was having its way with her. Just when it seemed her dread had stiffened enough for her to stop the tape and send it straight to the police without looking, Dr. Freedent removed something from his coat pocket. It was a small black cloth pouch. Immediately, he reached inside and pulled something out. At first, it was engulfed by the mass of his giant hand, and she could not see what it was. Then, she saw that it was just a simple matchbox. The dentist reached out toward her and placed it on the lower portion of her stomach. He then backed away.

Pauline's eyes scanned the television monitor with a glazed, numbing confusion. What was going to be the purpose of this horrible insanity? Or better said, what had been the purpose? She had been watching the screen as if it were a horror movie. This person on the screen was not her. This woman, this corpse lying loosely with its mouth disgustingly ajar looked nothing like the lovely woman she had noticed in the mirrors around her house. She wanted to scream at the woman, "Wake up! For God's sake, wake up!"

But the woman did not wake up. She lay silent beneath the amused glare of Freedent, his awkward hairy arms folded against his swollen prideful chest.

Nothing happened for what seemed like an eternity. The aching suspense nearly drove Pauline to advance the tape, when, in an instant, the matchbox began to shimmer with movement.

First, it shook slowly and then, more and more violently. Finally, a flap at the front broke loose, and the contents raced out several inches forward and stood completely still.

Pauline's eyes locked in horror at the apparatus of the dentist's madness.

A two-inch long cockroach was sitting on the middle of her stomach.

Her face collapsed into a helpless glare of shock. She was paralyzed to move as she watched the disgusting creature crawl clumsily over her chest and slowly work its way toward her neck.

"It's not real," she said out loud. "It's not real."

The cockroach began climbing slowly up the slope of her neck just beneath her chin and fell immediately back onto her soft, milky-white neck. Again and again, it tried and each time it fell back to where it had begun. It was simply too fat to climb.

After several more attempts, the cockroach made its way up the left side of her jaw. Pauline noticed that Freedent's arms were no longer folded. His hands were now clasped, and he wore an exceptionally wide grin.

Up her jaw the roach went. Then, finally, it slipped across her eye and proceeded eagerly around her pointed little nose. Pauline's mouth filled with vomit as the creature on the television aggressively plunged its head between her half open lips. Its legs flailed as it pushed deeper and deeper into her mouth. Finally, Freedent reached out and squeezed her cheeks hard, allowing the cockroach's swollen body to slip in completely.

Pauline turned away from the television. She could no longer contain the vomit in her mouth, and it spewed through her fingers and onto the floor. Over and over, she heaved as the image of the vile insect wriggled through her brain. Then, something happened that sent her over the edge.

Her vomit, which had been mostly clear to this point, now contained tiny brown apple seeds. Tiny, soft apple seeds. More and more began to show up in the vomit. Then, dozens of them began falling from her gaping mouth. For a moment, Pauline thought she was hallucinating. She had eaten no apples and even if she had, it would have taken dozens to generate this number of seeds. Then, she caught a glimpse of one of the seeds that had stuck to the sleeve on her left arm. It was moving. At once she knew. The brown, tender objects were not seeds at all. They were newborn roaches.

Pauline gave out a muffled scream and then began choking as more and more infant roaches piled onto the floor beneath her head. The ones that had been "born" first had now begun to scatter while some had attached themselves to her long blonde hair. Pauline let out another muffled cry and stumbled clumsily across her living room floor.

The agony of the ordeal began to take its toll, and finally she collapsed to the floor. Still, the roaches kept coming. It went on the same for several minutes until she could wretch no more. Then, the insects simply crawled independently up her throat and out of her mouth.

The burn in Pauline's throat was rivaled only by the searing pains in her gut. It felt like someone was stabbing her from the inside. Blood began to pool next to her face and, still, the roaches came. Out of the corner of her eye she could see that the Dr. Freedent on the television was now working on her tooth.

Pauline closed her eyes tightly and saw her father's face. His arms were reaching out to her. His face was the same sad one he had worn the day she had left home. Tears raced down her cheeks to mix with the newly birthed roaches on her chin.

Summoning what little strength the roaches had afforded her, Pauline staggered to her feet and moved dizzily to the front window. She opened it and draped her head lazily outside. She gazed sadly for a short time at the miniscule people hurrying below unsuspectingly. At least this time, she thought, they'll have the tape.

THE END

THE INVERTEBRATE

In the early years, the townsfolk harvested their finest crops and placed them at the edge of the woods in offering. And, when the season came, they sat in great circles with ardent prayers upon their trembling lips.

But The Invertebrate had no interest in such things, and when the townsfolk heard its shrill cries of hunger racketing across the thick lumbering forest, they knew it, and they scattered across the village square like insects exposed by the removal of some old, rotted log.

As their numbers thinned, the oldest of the town volunteered themselves as forfeit, and they hugged their families goodbye like soldiers bound to some hopeless war.

They stood at the place where the tree line skirted the field and held hands and sang hymns waiting for The Invertebrate to arrive. And they were united in their love of their families and their village. And this made them strong and fearless even in the face of such a grotesque annihilation.

But, when the trees cracked and bent away from each other, and they saw The Invertebrate's face, their legs folded beneath them like cardboard sticks.

It wrapped its muculent stump hands around their wastes and lifted them to its twitching insect face. It studied each of them with its bulging bundles of vacant sagging eyes. Whimpers leaked from their agonized mouths as it inhaled their scent with hot snorting whiffs. But their smell was the wasted essence of the old. And, The Invertebrate had no interest in such things. So, he cast them aside and continued toward the village on a glutinous track of steaming mucous.

Once, a fool-hearted army of men had charged into the woods, armed with poles shaved sharp at the ends. But, in the woods they stayed, and no one ever spoke of this, again.

There were rumors of other towns, but those who had set out to find them were frightened back by ogre-like grunting and a cascading thunder of snapping trees.

The slightest activity seemed to awaken The Invertebrate. So, all attempts at escape were forbidden. It was agreeable to everyone. Now, The Invertebrate only came with the season, and no one wanted to tempt it further.

It was agreed that the carnage could be blunted if offerings were placed along the treeline, and, so, a lottery came to be. Children were made exempt until the age of thirteen; but, as the men became scarce, this was lowered to ten.

And, when the season came, the townsfolk gathered in the square in the burnt orange morning light and drew small pieces of leather cut into geometric shapes. Then, one final piece was drawn and those who cupped the identical shape in their hands would weep, and their loved ones would howl with hopeless grief.

It was by such a procedure that a young girl was routed toward a destiny of doom. Aged ten, she surpassed the exemption just two weeks before; and, although, it felt unsavory, there was no doubting the legitimacy of her selection.

The girl's mother had slept poorly in the preceding nights, her mind clouded with haunting visions she was confident would be made true. And her faith in this helped her prepare. And so when it came to pass, she held the girl with a dry face devoid of emotion. The girl didn't cry either, and while others found this curious, her mother knew it to be consistent with her nature.

They knew from experience that it was best to tie the lottery winners to the posts right after their selection to avoid ambitions of self-preservation. And, so, all four were carried to the edge of the woods and fastened to warped wooden poles, stuck deep into the ground and spaced six feet apart.

The prayer was brief, and all the while, the prayer-leader glanced over his shoulder as if The Invertebrate might be bearing down on him from behind. The somber goodbyes had all been delivered in the village square. And, so, all of the townsfolk turned and ventured home in hopes that the flesh-loaded posts would satisfy The Invertebrate's lust.

There were two middle-aged women to the girl's right, and to theirs, a young viral man the townsfolk had hated to lose. The women stared out into the woods, eyes wide as dinner plates and webbed with bright red veins from crying. The man had vomited when they'd tied his hands behind the pole and now his shirt stank of a sour bile.

Their lips moved with rapid prayer, but their words were swept away by the chilled rolling winds. When they heard the first sharp sounds of splintering tree trunks, they shrieked involuntarily through gaping oval mouths.

All except for the girl whose sea-green eyes peered forward eerily through a tiny face that seemed made of stone. And the fearless expression was no mask. For she knew that The Invertebrate was fallible, as all things are. And she knew it, because she had once seen it many months before.

When she saw it, she was gathering stones from a dry pond near the river where the woods licked at the fields. The rocks there had tiny flecks of minerals in them, and they sparkled in the sunlight like bits of hot glitter. She had plucked at least a dozen from the white dusty ground, when she saw The Invertebrate bobbing in the shadows just inside the trees. A gush of fear ran over her body, and she let the stones fall.

She turned to run, but her feet seemed fastened to the ground. The Invertebrate looked at her with a bundle of crowded glassy eyes. Its mouth opened and a pitchy shriek poured out through dripping strings of mucous. Her legs collapsed beneath her, and she just sat there in the middle of the dried pond, watching the true size of the creature ooze around the trees and re-coagulate in the open space in front of her.

It stunk like a heap of festering flesh, and it slid forward on its giant glutinous pad with a sloppy drooling eagerness that filled her with incomprehensible terror. But, when it touched the crusty edges of the dried pond, it made a terrible noise and reared back like a stallion over a rattlesnake. A haze of evaporate steamed from the part of its body that had touched the pale dust, and it turned and crashed into the forest in a blinding anguish.

She sat there weeping for a long time. And, then she got up to go home. But, first, she plunged her hands into the pale earth and piled fistfuls of the grainy dust into the pockets of her dress. And there it remained until this moment. None squandered. Every single grain still in place.

The Invertebrate was much larger than the others had expected. And, when the two women saw it, they screamed. The Invertebrate studied the four pink fleshy offerings, and pools of saliva gathered beneath its massive tubular lips. The man had defecated when he saw it, but

The Invertebrate didn't seem to mind. It puckered its lips around his head and popped it loose like a berry from a bush. Then, it positioned its mouth around the neck hole and slurped out all the blood and organs like a vacuum.

The women went insane with terror as they watched the man's hollow skin and bones flop to the earth in an awkward heap. The Invertebrate consumed them quickly in an orderly deliberate sequence on its way to the girl, but when it turned to face her, it paused for a moment as if in recognition.

The girl's hands were tied loosely, as her mother had said it would be, and she slipped them free with little fuss. The Invertebrate watched as she strode in front of it with a champion's swagger. Then, it lifted the front of its massive body into the air and howled so loudly she thought the trees might split in two.

She stood completely still as The Invertebrate's sucking mouth descended over her body like a billowy net over a tiny butterfly. But, at the last moment she pushed her hands into her pockets and stripped out a choking cloud of powdery white dust.

The Invertebrate's face dissolved against the ashy plumes like a melting marshmallow, and a yellow foam sizzled from the wounded areas. It tried to recoil, but its eyes were melted shut and without them, it could only sulk backward and flop around in a blind fury.

The girl approached The Invertebrate and cast the remaining powder on the rest of its body. The whole thing swelled like a great balloon until holes burst out all over, and it liquefied into a bubbling mushy goop. Later, when she led the townsfolk to the muck puddle, a lot of people cried.

The mother and the girl left the town soon after, but her memory lived in the village for many years. They talked of God and sacrifice, and of true miracles which could only come from children who were too young to know that they were impossible.

THE END

THE NATURAL HIGH

Derrick jammed two of the berries into his mouth and crushed them to mush. He shut his eyes and waited for something to happen.

"I told you," Booker said. "You have to swallow them, or it doesn't work."

He gave him two more, and Derrick gulped them whole nearly gagging on the size.

"Do you feel anything yet?" Booker said.

Derrick didn't answer. Almost immediately he had felt the warm rush Booker and Eddie had described.

"He feels it," Eddie said. "Give me some more!"

Booker jerked the bag away.

"I told you, the first two are free and then it's a buck apiece."

Eddie crammed his hand into his left pocket and yanked out two crumpled one-dollar bills. He pushed them into Booker's outstretched hand.

"Alright, Gimme."

Booker reached into the ragged brown paper bag and removed two plump yellow berries. They were engorged with juices, and it appeared it would take very little to make one pop.

Eddie devoured them with voracity, and the warm rush was upon him again.

Derrick was lying on his back kicking at the air.

Later, when the effects had died out, the three boys began walking home. As usual, their stomachs ached. But it was worth it. None of them would question that. It was worth it, and it wasn't even close.

"You've got to tell me where you find those things," Eddie said. He was clutching his swollen belly like the other boys.

"Heck, no," Booker said. "You'd just go eat them all at once and kill yourself. And then there wouldn't be any left for us."

Booker dug his elbow into Derrick's side, and the two laughed.

"Man, what kind of friend charges his buds for something he finds growing in some field somewhere?" Eddie whined.

That was funny coming from Eddie. In the 17 years they had all been on Earth, he had screwed both Booker and Derrick over on everything from Halloween candy to girls to beer.

The three stopped outside Derrick's house.

"You sure those things won't hurt you?" he asked.

"Man, quit being such a Mary," Booker said. "I told you, I've been eating them for over two weeks, and I feel fine."

Derrick had been the last to try the berries. When Booker had first shown up with a fistful of them, Eddie had nearly swallowed his hand. But Derrick was nervous, and he refused to try any. But a week of listening to the two other boys rave about the feeling finally wore him down.

Booker hocked a wad of spit into the dirt.

"The stomachache will go away after about an hour, and you'll be fine."

But Derrick's stomachache didn't go away, and later that night while his parents were sleeping, he went into the bathroom and wretched. He was in there for a long time and when the toilet was nearly filled with gobs of mucus and bits of his mother's goulash, something strange happened. The two berries came up.

Derrick studied them. Amazingly, they appeared just as they had when he had swallowed them. His digestive juices had done nothing to alter their appearance. Out of pure curiosity he reached his fingers into the muck and removed one of the juicy balls. He flipped it around in his hand. There were no marks, and it was just as firm as it had originally been. There was, however, an extremely small hole on the bottom. He picked up the other and looked it over. It was the same.

Derrick dropped the berries back into the toilet and flushed it. He brushed his teeth and went back to bed.

The next morning, he raced through the kitchen door without breakfast. He never ate breakfast anymore. His mother hated it, but there was no point to arguing any longer. Derrick was well on his way to the lifestyle of his father and his father's father. He was bullheaded would not listen to a woman. Not even the one that admitted him into the world.

Derrick rushed out the door and found Eddie waiting outside. He was wearing brand new white converse shoes. Derrick dashed out to meet him.

"Pretty sweet, huh?" Eddie said. "Got 'em last night for my birthday."

"They'd be great if they weren't white," Derrick prodded. "You'll never keep them clean."

Eddie stared down at his feet for a few moments before shaking off the remarks.

"Jealousy is a bitter pill, Derrick. You should be happy for your friends and their success even if your life sucks by comparison."

Derrick's eyes circled in his head, and the two headed toward school. They were thick in the marrow of an argument about gambling and football when Booker met them about thirty feet in front of the school.

"What are you two Nancys bitching about?"

His face was red and bloated and his usually flat and muscular stomach was round and distended.

"Whoa," Eddie gasped. "What the hell is wrong with you?"

Booker coughed up what sounded like a grand amount of phlegm and spat it out behind him.

"I'm fine. Got a cold or something. I'll tell you one thing; I can't handle sitting through classes all day."

"What do you have in mind?" Eddie's interest was secured.

"What say I take you boys down to where I get the berries, and we hang out all day getting fucked up?"

He wore a frail smile on his face, and it looked to Derrick like he probably had a hell of a fever.

"Hell ya!" Eddie rejoiced.

"I don't know," Derrick stuttered. "You don't look so good. Maybe it's from those berries. They made me sick last night, and that was the first time I'd ever eaten them. Who knows what they might have done to you after all this time?"

Booker flung a look of rage at Derrick that even made Eddie take half-step back. Booker was the most intimidating person either of them had ever known and was pretty much notorious as the "bad influence" of the group in the presumptions of the elders in town. And they were far from wrong. Virtually every destructive idea the three of them converted into reality began as a baby in Booker's brain. If someone's windows ended up shattered or their car interior was torched, they could reasonably surmise that Booker had drawn up the blueprints.

The majority of time, Derrick went along out of sheer fear of Booker's discontent. Eddie seemed to just go along too. Although, it seemed to Derrick that Eddie's relish for rebellion was a competent rival to Booker's.

"I told you, there's nothing wrong with those goddamn berries. I'm tired of hearing you wine and complain."

He hawked up another ball of jelly from his throat and did away with it.

"Me and Eddie are going." His eyes bore deep into Derrick's. "Are you coming?"

Derrick swallowed hard and just went along.

The two boys followed Booker toward the familiar dusty trail that led to the abandoned baseball yard where they used to play their little league games when they were young boys.

They had all been on the same team and the wins and losses solidified their friendship. Derrick had been a pitcher, and Booker was the catcher. Eddie played outfield and there was another, Marcus, who played first base. They were all inseparable for better or for worse. And then Marcus drowned at one of his family reunions when he was 15, leaving the other three boys to make up for the havoc he might have wrought.

"How'd you find this, Booker?" Eddie asked. "What were you doing at the old ball field?"

Booker's lungs were struggling to keep up with his legs. He stopped and waited for them to catch up before answering.

"I don't know," he gasped. "I just come here sometimes, alright?"

He turned his back and began walking again.

Booker led them through a large tree line that passed behind the right field of the ball yard. A few steps later, they crossed a shallow creek and found themselves at the foot of a remarkably steep green hill.

"How the hell do we get up this?" Eddie whined.

Booker reached into the tall bright grass that carpeted the hill and exposed a rope. It was thick and brown, and it was riddled with knots each tied about a foot apart. It led about 50 feet to the summit of the miniature green mountain. He wrapped a piece of it around his wrist and jammed his right foot into the foundation of the hill.

"Let's go," he said hoarsely.

Derrick and Eddie looked at each other and then, one after the other, they followed him up the lime-colored slant. The incline was even more abrupt than Derrick had judged, and his feet struggled to negotiate a footing in the slippery grass.

When he finally reached the top and rose to his feet, he saw an average-sized tree littered with yellow bulbs of fruit. The trunk of the tree was black and so were the leaves. It sat alone amongst the grass atop the strange hill. Derrick's stomach began to twist as he watched Eddie and Booker rip handfuls of the berries from the tree's branches and stuff them into their mouths.

Derrick sat on the ground and watched them. Booker appeared to have a wondrous fascination with the fingers on his left hand. Eddie just giggled and writhed in the grass.

Derrick found it difficult to resist the urge to eat the berries himself. He longed for the tremendous feeling of well-being. It was a sensation that would have been difficult for any of them to explain. The best way to say it was that it was like a full-body itch that actually felt good. Or maybe a pleasure so great that it bordered on pain.

It didn't matter anymore. The thought of Booker's distended belly and those little dark holes in the bottom of the berries he had vomited up diminished his appetite for the juicy yellow balls.

When the feeling finally passed, and the other two boys had quieted down, Derrick walked over to Eddie and helped him up.

"Man, that was the best one so far," he said through his slobbering lips.

Booker hadn't gotten up yet, and the two of them walked to where he lay. His eyes were closed, and his belly was more bloated than ever.

"Booker," Derrick said. "You o.k.?"

His eyes opened, and he coughed violently.

"I feel horrible," he gasped. The color of his face had advanced from red to purple, and his entire body was engulfed with sweat. The other boys looped their arms under each of his and hoisted him to his feet. Booker burst out a shrill squall and collapsed back into the grass. He began tossing all over the ground, and Eddie began to panic.

"What the hell is wrong with him?" he asked. "Is it those berries? Is that going to happen to me?"

Derrick told him to shut up. He put his hand on Booker's head. It was blistering.

"Booker, what's wrong?" he asked. "What do we do?"

Thin streams of vomit trickled from sides of Booker's mouth, and his words were difficult to interpret.

"My stomach," it sounded like. "My stomach."

Ripe teakettle screams exploded from his mouth, sending Derrick and Eddie stumbling backward. Booker raised his shirt to unveil the inflated gut beneath it. Derrick's mouth fell agape, and Eddie began to scream. His distended gut undulated, as if hundreds of little fingers stretched against the skin from the inside.

"What the hell?" Eddie moaned. "Is that going to happen to me? Is that going to happen to me?"

Suddenly a small dark spot appeared at the top of his belly and began lengthening downward into what looked like a seam. His stomach stretched at the sides, and the seam burst open. Hundreds of finger-sized eel-like creatures wiggled toward the light.

Eddie's screams were nearly as deafening as Booker's. The creatures immediately began to poor out of the cavity that was once Booker's stomach. Amazingly, Booker had retained consciousness, and he began to flick at them with his hand as they squirmed toward his head. A swarm of them clung to his fingers, and he shook his hands violently. His fingers were gone in an instant, and the tiny eels continued their feeding frenzy up his muscular arms and then onto his shoulders.

Derrick's stomach crumpled itself into knots as he watched Booker either lose consciousness or die. It didn't matter either way, because a few minutes later, a large pile of eel-worms was all that remained. They hadn't left a single piece of Booker. Not even the bones. The only physical evidence of his existence now ran through the digestive tracts of the slimy black things born from his stomach.

Derrick spun to look at Eddie, but he had already turned to run. He fled to edge of the precipitous green decline and bailed off. Derrick ran to the edge and watched as he banged and flopped head over heels to the bottom. He jumped to his feet and limped quickly toward the ball field. Derrick thought it looked like he had broken an arm. But that was the least of his problems, he supposed.

He turned and looked back at the spot where the eel-worms had consumed Booker. There were only a few left now. It appeared the rest of them had slithered off into the bushes. Derrick shivered as he looked up at the tree, still rich with ripe yellow berries. He reached beneath him for the rope and began climbing down the hill.

That night, Derrick said little to his mother at dinner, but this was nothing new. Later, he lay in bed abstaining from sleep. Booker's gruesome ordeal lay at the forefront of his mind. But few of his thoughts related to pity for Booker. He thought instead about the berries he had vomited up, the two holes in the bottoms and the words Eddie kept screaming as the eel-worms feasted on their friend.

"Is this going to happen to me?"

Derrick and Eddie didn't speak for the next several days. Derrick came down with a convenient cold that granted him a few days at home from school. He had heard that Eddie had too. He had heard this from his mother who happened to be close friends with Eddie's mom. Long ago, the two had thought it a good idea to put their two sons in little league together so they could be friends, but now Derrick knew his mom secretly regretted it.

A few days into his cold, Derrick heard through this grapevine that Eddie's cold was getting worse. Then a few days later than that, he learned that Eddie's mom was furious because he had actually sneaked out one night after his mother had measured his temperature at 102 degrees. But that wasn't the part that irked her, his mother said. The worst part was the pile of worms he had left under the covers as some sort of immature joke.

Derrick's mother ranted about Eddie and Booker and swore the three would never be allowed together again. Derrick let her vent without interrupting. Then he got up and went to his bedroom.

Later that night, he felt something swimming in his belly while he was reading comic books in bed. He raised his shirt to see his stomach shimmering. He went to the kitchen and extracted a sharp steak knife from one of the drawers. He slowly went upstairs and closed his bedroom door. He lay on the bed and waited patiently. There would be two, he thought. He could hear his mother downstairs laughing at some show on the television. He laid the knife across his chest and closed his eyes.

THE END

THE GIRL WHO LIVED

In the morning, Claire awoke to a beautiful silence, the real world crystallizing slowly as she lifted from her dreams. Soon, a hard knocking shattered it all apart, and her heart picked up as reality seized her mind. She put on her robe and answered the door. A soldier stood before her, his face unfamiliar and very young.

"You have one hour," he said, before turning his back.

She shut the door and hurried to the bathroom for a quick shower. Without delay, she dried and dressed her body in clothing that seemed appropriate enough for a diversity of outcomes. As the soldier pounded the door, she quickly applied enough makeup to give her pallid face a touch of life. Then she left the room and joined him in the hallway.

They made their way through the appropriate passages and elevators until they arrived topside, where they met more soldiers, who guided her out of the facility and into the open air. High away in the pale blue sky, the sun flared brightly, its forgotten warmth so nourishing to her ivory skin. She looked at it for an instant, and it seemed to look back, a floral wind kicking up to celebrate the reunion.

"Hello," said Dominic Betancur. He wore safari gear and he approached wearing the smile of a lunatic. "Please, join me in the lead vehicle."

She nodded politely and followed him, Romero watching them the whole way before climbing into a separate truck.

They left the compound and drove out into the surrounding flats. Claire studied the landscape through the open window, the grasses low and wispy, the horizon mostly bare. After two hours of this, they crossed into a strange and wasted land, with black skeletal trees that stuck from the ground like the curled ends of burned matchsticks.

Claire glanced out her window at the desolate scrub and contemplated the scant chance of life in all that dirt and sparsity. But before she got far, a family of little rabbits shot out from a distant bur shrub, their tiny footwork kicking up faint puffs of white sand that rose up in the clear air and then vanished, like little explosions of powder on some enormous expression of still life.

Dominic smiled.

"I've seen amazing things in this area," he said. "Mother Nature finds a way."

By the time the great wall of jungle flora appeared on the horizon, the sun had pulled near the earth. As its burn dulled, all makes of orange light shot through the flowing treetops, while great birds circled like giant insects above them. Together, the birds moved in perfect agreement, congealing into enormous black halos that swelled and undulated in some sort of ancient unanimity, which seemed sinister to Claire at such a distance for reasons that were beyond her will to understand.

As they approached, the wild thicket seemed to grow before their eyes, and soon they saw the dark gape that tunneled into it. They followed the road forward, the trucks like motorized toys before the flora's girth. With a bump, the vehicles pierced the jungle's edge, a thick darkness embracing them, a sudden swell of insect chatter and hooting animals booming out from every direction.

As they pressed further, their headlights bored into the obscurity, the fog concealing what lay ahead, as it tumbled over the uneven road. Every so often, animals would bolt across the path, their eyes like bright little fire balls, glinting and glimmering and then quickly disappearing into the smothering black.

Big, bulging tree roots stuck out of the road like python snakes, and as the tires thumped over them, Claire's hand clutched the door handle and then Dominic's knee by mistake. He smiled and leaned toward her, his nostrils taking an audible sniff of her hair.

"Don't worry," he said. "We're well-equipped for this terrain."

She moved away from him with care and settled in her seat. His demeanor seemed much the same despite her detachment, and after a while, he closed his eyes and fell asleep. They pressed on into the jungle, traveling in silence for hours. She tried to stay alert, but her eyelids took on more and more weight, and soon she fell asleep beside him, the jostling carriages doing little to disturb the depth of her slumber.

In her dreams, she saw her little mother all dressed in black alone beside a casket. As Claire watched from above, the old woman wrung her withered hands and wept, as she looked upon the face of her dead husband. Claire called out louder and louder, but her mother could not hear. And after a while, she collapsed and died and turned to ash beneath her clothing, such a vision jerking Claire awake in her seat, the sun flaring considerately outside the window glass.

She immediately noticed the changed terrain. They'd exited the jungle and fell upon a paved road, which ran neatly along a picturesque coastline, where rolling waves spilled over a jagged, rocky shore. Dominic slept beside her, his mouth agape, saliva seeping out its corners. She nudged him and his eyes popped open.

"Have we arrived?" he asked.

"I don't think so," she said.

He sat up and ran his hands through his hair.

"Oh, good," he said, as he peered out the windows. "It won't be long now."

They drove another two hours before she saw the buildings stick up over the horizon and then another hour before the little city manifested around them. Soon, they joined traffic and traffic jams, and the soldiers held guns out the windows until the cars scurried to the side and let them pass. The vehicles rumbled through the streets, like armored trucks pregnant with gold bars, and people fled the roads and gathered upon the sidewalks, as if something presidential had mysteriously joined their ranks.

They continued through the streets, slowing at intersections only for a moment before rushing through red lights, and then they finally arrived at their destination: a pair of lofty twin ivory pillars that provided luxury accommodation for some of the wealthiest of the region. The trucks wheeled around the backside of the buildings and descended into an underground parking facility, then they finally came to a stop, and the engines fell silent. Dominic opened his door and stretched his legs.

"That was quite a trip," he said, as he rubbed his lower back. He snapped his fingers at one of the soldiers, who quickly approached Claire and helped her from the vehicle. A short, well-dressed bald man came scurrying from the elevator, his tiny eyes peering out from behind a pair of round, designer eyeglasses.

"Mr. Betancur, I'm so happy to see you've arrived," he said. He offered a tiny, feminine-looking hand and it disappeared within Dominic's.

"Hello, Paul. I trust everything is arranged?"

"Yes, sir. We've seen to all your requirements."

"Good."

Dominic turned to Claire.

"Romero will escort you to your room, where you'll have an opportunity to freshen up. We'll reconnect later for dinner and some entertainment." He smiled and took her hand. "I'm looking forward to our evening together."

He raised her hand to his lips and kissed it. Then he turned and followed Paul to the elevator with five soldiers in tow.

"This way, Ms. Foley," Romero said, as the lone remaining soldier fell in at his side. The three approached a second elevator and took it to the lobby floor. After a few seconds, the door opened to show the lobby mostly empty, save for two tanned businessmen who looked upon the three of them with audacious curiosity.

When they approached the front desk, Romero gave Dominic's name, which brought a keycard and several submissive smiles, and then the three took the elevator up several stories, where they found Claire's room.

"Mr. Lopez will remain outside your door for your protection," Romero said before turning to take the elevator back to wherever he was going. Claire eyed the soldier for a moment and then shut the door.

She turned to assess the room, the walls tan, bedding burgundy, the whole setup as beautiful as any she'd ever seen. She walked over to the sink and filled a cup of water. She drank it down and refilled it again, repeating this twice more and then dropping the cup into the sink. She approached the bed and collapsed upon it, immediately falling into a dreamless sleep. In what seemed like only a few minutes' time, someone began rapping the door, but when she awoke to see the clock, she realized she had been asleep for more than three hours.

"Ms. Foley," Romero called from outside.

She sat up and glanced about the room. The woman in the mirror looked at her through nervous eyes. She straightened her posture and adjusted her expression until the reflection gained her approval. Then she crossed the room and opened the door.

"Yes?"

Romero straightened when he saw her.

"Mr. Betancur has arranged dinner reservations for seven o'clock."

He looked her over from head to toe.

"You'll find suitable attire in your closet. I'll wait outside while you prepare and then I'll escort you to his car."

Claire nodded and shut the door.

Over the next hour, she showered and prepared her hair and makeup, hands working in an automated sort of way, an expressionless face staring back from the mirror as she worked.

The form-fitting black dress they'd selected on her behalf fit remarkably, as if they'd crept in and tailored it around her body as she slept. When she'd finished, she looked well-suited to the role she might play on this particular evening, in this particular setting for this particular man. And when she opened the door to greet Romero and his associate, both men seemed a little startled by what they saw.

"This way," Romero said. The three crossed the hall and entered the elevator, a staggering silence ushering them along. In the lobby, they found Dominic waiting, a broad smile stretching across his face at the sight of Claire in her new dress.

"You look outstanding," he said, as he clasped his hands together. "I picked this out myself, and what a job I did."

She forced a smile.

"Where are we going?"

He shook his head while clicking his tongue against the roof of his mouth.

"Everything is a surprise this evening." He smiled and put his hands over her bare shoulders. "Relax, you're off the clock. Enjoy yourself."

They left the hotel in a limousine, two of the soldiers with them, each dressed in dark suits.

Outside Claire's window, the little city brimmed with electricity, vibrant neon signs glowing warm and brightly amid a diversity of human beings. Lured by every imaginable trapping, people entered and exited strange looking venues, some of these places bold and obvious along the street, others low and hidden down narrow steps that burrowed below the city's surface.

As the limo worked through traffic, she saw all manner of buskers doing all manner of tricks, their inverted hats beside them, gathering up bills and coins of varying denominations. People gathered around the performers with clapping hands and big, affected eyes, their attention swayed only by the prostitutes, who whispered sweet promises in ear after ear, while tickling with gentle hands the insides of thighs.

They approached an intersection and idled before a single red stop light, which dangled from a wire which hung loosely across the road. As they waited, Claire surveyed the neighboring vehicles, cab drivers beeping their horns at crossing pedestrians, smart cars like toys next to monstrous trucks, which rumbled and shook, as they belched dark smoke from their rears.

Soon, the light turned green, and the limo pressed forward with the rest of traffic. For a time, they cooperated with the flow, moving slowly and stopping, as the vehicles choked the streets. At last, Dominic summoned the driver with the intercom.

"Somchai, go ahead and take the outer roads," he said.

"Sir?" said the driver.

"It's perfectly alright, Somchai. Go ahead now."

The driver hooked a quick left down a dark, narrow street and accelerated past the guttersnipe, which eyed the gleaming black vehicle through wild, bloodshot eyes. Dominic looked at Claire.

"The city is well protected on its interior," he said. "On the outer streets, however, things are more uncertain. Most know better than to molest this vehicle. On the other hand, there are some degenerates who are either desperate or ignorant enough to make a mistake."

He put a hand on her knee.

"You needn't worry, though. This vehicle is impervious to gunfire, and I can have a hundred well-armed men at my disposal in a matter of minutes."

She looked down at his hand and then up to his face.

"That's good, I suppose."

He smiled and nodded.

"Indeed."

He removed his hand and sat back in his seat, while the limo navigated a series of turns that led them away from traffic. Soon the lighting turned faint and the roads grew choppy, as they entered shanty neighborhoods, where shadowy figures scuttled about in the darkness. Finally, they pushed through these discouraging areas and emerged on a lonely road, which ran a circle around the unlit edges of the city. Outside, a great pale moon hung low and heavy over the barren landscape, where scattered vegetation stuck up sharply from the dry, dusty ground.

"Lower the window," Dominic said to one of the soldiers.

"I'm not sure that's a good idea, sir," the soldier replied.

Dominic lowered his eyebrows.

"It's a fine idea."

The soldier nodded.

"I'm sorry, sir. Of course."

He lowered the window, and a flood of warm air filtered its way into the vehicle. A pungent floral aroma permeated their nostrils, though Claire could not identify its source out in the thin, pale light. One of the soldiers sneezed repeatedly into a handkerchief.

"I'm sorry."

Dominic watched the man as he attempted to gather himself.

"Perhaps we should shut the windows," Claire said.

Dominic frowned.

"That won't be necessary."

He summoned the driver through the intercom.

"Somchai, please pull over for a moment."

The limousine crept to a halt, while the soldier's face contorted oddly against another fearsome sneeze.

"Please join Somchai up front," said Dominic.

The soldier nodded.

"Of course."

He opened the door and exited, leaving Dominic and the remaining soldier alone with Claire.

"Was that absolutely necessary?" Claire asked, as the vehicle pulled forward.

Dominic shrugged.

"Very few things are absolutely necessary," said Dominic. "In any case, the fresh air invigorates me. Don't you find it invigorating?"

She shrugged.

"It's fine, yes."

They drove on, the vehicle jerking occasionally against the old broken road, its passengers clutching the seats to steady their jostled bodies. Finally, the limo made a sharp turn and pushed back into civilization, where strange, ambiguous faces peered out from the dark edges of the road. Claire watched as tall shadows stretched out from the city's center, which glittered with all makes of lighting that were welcome and missed. Soon, her body began to relax at the illusion of safety, though in her heart she recognized it as such.

When they arrived at their first destination, a very excited-looking Asian man met them on the street. He addressed Dominic in French, his demeanor humble and polite. They exchanged pleasantries and then they entered the restaurant where they were seated amid others of similar stature.

Claire settled in her seat.

"This is the premier dining venue within 500 miles," Dominic said, his eyebrows resting high upon his forehead.

Claire offered a smile.

"It looks it."

Dominic nodded.

"Well, in this case, looks are not deceiving."

They sat in silence for a moment and then a tall, thin waiter approached the table.

"How are you this evening?" he asked. Dominic put a finger up and replied in French.

"Oui," the waiter said. He turned and walked away.

"Do you speak French?" Dominic asked Claire.

"No," she lied.

Soon their table overflowed with an array of foods, over which not a single one she had a say. She ate sparingly while taking notice of the restaurant staff, their faces painted with disgust, Dominic seeming oblivious to this along with many other things.

"Wealth has its privileges," he said, as he forced a slab of liver into his cheeks. "People seek it like children to fireflies. Their arms flailing, eyes tracing a glimmer here, a glimmer there."

Claire stirred her food with an odd-looking fork.

"But is that what they really want?" Dominic asked. He waited for a response. "No," he continued. "It is most certainly not."

Claire dropped her fork and looked up.

"What is it, then, that people want?" she asked flatly.

Dominic smiled.

"I'd like to know your opinion."

"Happiness," she said. "People want to be happy."

He smirked, as if he'd pulled the string on an elaborate trap.

"People say they want to be happy, but it's not true. Not even remotely." He leaned back in his chair and folded his hands on his lap. "They know the things that would make them happy: a new job, exercise, reading, eating better, spending more time with their children, things they write on pieces of paper, things they can only manage for a day or two. But they don't follow through with any of them. Instead, every day, they take specific steps to promote unhappiness, because happiness is not what they really want."

Claire leaned back in her chair.

"What do they really want then?"

"Stimulation, of course," he said. "This is the only thing anyone really wants. It's what drives husbands and wives into the arms of others, what makes people drink, smoke. It's why people eat fast food, play sports, play video games, read, drive fast, jump out of airplanes, buy new clothes. My goodness, it's even why people get angry."

Claire rubbed her eye.

"Why they get angry?"

"Of course," he said, as he folded his hands together. "Anger is the perfect form of stimulation, because it makes people feel powerful. It's an antidote to anxiety, to fear. It allows you to say the things you've always wanted to say to those people of whom you're most afraid. You stand up for yourself, put people in their rightly deserved places. It's an artificial form of power. It creates drive."

He withdrew a cigarette and lit it, the staff taking notice without interfering.

"It's also about the only form of stimulation you can easily generate yourself," he said. "It's really no problem. Just think about that specific something or someone, and you're there."

Claire leaned forward, the gravity of the argument dissolving her angst.

"I think most people view anger as toxic," she said. "Few would equate it with happiness."

Dominic grinned.

"But that's the point," he said. "People don't want to be happy. Why else would a person toss and turn in bed at night embracing feelings of jealousy and rage? These things happen. They say, well, I can't control my thoughts. Of course, that's not true. The other thoughts are boring. The angry thoughts are stimulating. That's why they're so addictive."

He sat up.

"Let me paint the picture," he said, as he furrowed his brow. "You wake up in the morning feeling sad, helpless. What can you do about it? Not much most of the time. But within minutes, you can find your feet by conjuring up a good bit of anger. Before you know it, you're walking with a confidence, a swagger. You're stimulated. It's easy. Wake up sad or depressed? Get angry about something. People do it all the time without knowing it. Every day, they read the news, looking for stories that will set them off. They want it. They scan headlines searching for it. They want to be mad at someone. At the world."

Claire shook her head.

"That's not what I want."

Dominic pointed at her.

"Exactly. The world could use more like you. Or, better yet, more of you."

He smoked his cigarette and tilted his chin upward to exhale.

"But sadly, you will die, just like the rest of us. But you will leave children behind, yes?"

She said nothing.

"Oh, that's right, you have no children. What a pity."

He brought his cigarette to his lips and then stopped short.

"When people such as you die, it is a tragedy for humankind. And this, you will change through your research. You will remove the expiration date from human life and give humanity the gift of endless longevity."

She peered at him through caving eyelids.

"Humanity? You mean if my research yields a cure for aging, you would share it with humanity? Or would you keep it for certain people? People with money? People with power?"

He shook his head slowly.

"The gift of eternal or even extended life is not for the masses. It's not like clean water or medicine, which anyone should be entitled to. This thing we talk about must be kept from the ordinary, the people who would waste it, abuse it to taint the world with more of themselves, exhaust its resources and for what?"

Claire furrowed her brows.

"Kept for whom?"

"For those who have spent their lives contributing with their minds, people we need more of."

She took up her fork and stirred her cold food.

"Think about it," he said. "How much different might this world be if we had someone such as Einstein for even just another 30 years? Instead, we get hordes of ignorant people, mass-producing with six, seven, nine children. It's a downward spiral. The worst of us growing in numbers. The best of us becoming rarer and rarer by the decade."

He smoked again and then crushed his cigarette out on an empty plate.

"That sounds like passive intellectual genocide," she said. "Would you have administered polio vaccines based on a person's I.Q.?"

"Don't be ridiculous," he said. "This is the only practical way to employ our coming discovery."

She stirred faster.

"Just think about it, Claire. You're far smarter than I. This world is already too small for its current burden. What you suggest is to increase that burden. You speak of endless life. A world where people never age, where they live without disease, without diabetes, without pancreatic cancer or heart disease."

He withdrew another cigarette and set it afire.

"What comes next is starvation, land wars, laws over procreation. Who can have children, when, and how many? Society is forever changed. We lose everything."

He put his fist down on the table and the silverware rattled.

"No. We preserve our way of life by withholding this thing. We crack Pandora's Box just slightly to siphon its gifts, without unleashing a plague upon the world. Without ending it entirely."

He sucked his cigarette and watched her.

"Dominic," she said flatly. "I could debate you. But what's the point? Why do you even care what I think? I know you will do whatever you will, with or without my approval. I know I have no choice but to fulfill my obligation and make this thing you want. And I know it's only meant for those who can procure it through means of money or power. I know all these things and yet I still have no choice but to do as you wish. Why waste your time preaching this nonsense to me? What does it matter what I think?"

He pursed his lips and summoned the waiter, who delivered a check and quickly walked away.

"In time, I believe you will see things as I do," he said, as he placed five hundred American dollars on the table. "You are one of the brightest people we've ever had at our facility, and I want you to consider staying on after your term has expired."

Her eyes trickled upward to meet his.

"I'm only interested in getting back to my mother and my life."

He gave a polite smile.

"If that is what you wish, that is what you will have. But, again, I believe you may feel differently in time."

With that, he stood.

"Let's move on, now. I've made other arrangements for the evening."

They left the restaurant just as they arrived, the two sitting next to each other in the limousine, the soldiers across from them, their eyes vacant, minds seemingly elsewhere. When they reached their next destination, a short, bald man raced to open the car door.

"Mr. Betancur, it is our privilege to have you this evening," he said, without acknowledging Claire. "We have some of our finest ladies performing tonight. I hope you enjoy the show."

Dominic shook the man's hand, and they followed him through the door. Inside, a crowd of well-dressed people stood shoulder to shoulder before a large, empty stage. He placed them at a center table and gave a polite bow as he left. Claire evaluated the room. It was large and dark and only slightly illuminated by low bursts of orange incandescent lamps that glowed here and there, turning the guests into featureless silhouettes that spoke to one another in all manners of foreign tongue.

"I'd like to visit the bar," Claire said. "Is that o.k.?"

"Of course," Dominic said with a smile.

She stood and crossed the room, weaving through a crowd of well-dressed men, their necks whipping back toward her, as if towed by some exotic gravity.

She lured the bartender over and ordered a drink. When it came, she sipped from it lovingly, the alcohol sifting through her vasculature, warming her body. She saw a man in an expensive suit eying her from down the bar, his jaw square, a boyish smirk bleeding from the corner of his lips. She finished her drink and raised her hand to the bartender, but before she could summon him, the lights winked out, and the place erupted in noise.

She turned her body with all the rest, as splashes of red light soaked the stage. The first performer strutted forward, the thumping speakers at pace with every step.

The girl wore a black, strappy corset, her breasts spilling over the top like great jiggling boulders. The crowd gasped as she approached the chrome pole, which jutted from the stage floor like an ill-placed support column. In an instant, she scaled the thing and wrapped her legs around the cold metal, her long black hair spilling downward as she leaned back, the line of her cleavage square to the crowd. As her fans applauded, she traveled the pole with a practiced sexuality that seemed new and fresh and just for you. When it was over, she left the stage to an explosion of whistles and cheers.

A train of performers followed, each more talented than the last, each costume more colorful, more revealing. As the girls played their roles, energy built and flowed through the room, the men driven to the brink by the brazen display of sexual confidence, some of the girls winking shyly, others flexing and stomping the floor.

Finally, a beautiful red-headed girl took the stage. Last and most anticipated, she drew a prolonged introduction from the announcer and a ruckus from the crowd. As the lights flickered pink, she took the stage as if it were built just for her, drawing another girl forward by a leash affixed to a vinyl neck collar. The room became feverous as she teased and tempted the young thing with tickles from a feather and sharp lashes from a leather flogging whip. Soon, she was rid of the younger girl, banishing her from the stage with a stern slap to the face. Then she commanded everything: the stage, the crowd, time.

When it was over, the lights picked up a bit, and many of the guests filtered out. Claire stood up on her high heels and wobbled a little, her mind swimming under the influence of several cocktails. A strong hand took her arm and steadied her.

"Are you alright?" Dominic asked.

"Yes," Claire said, as she stripped her arm away. "Thank you."

"Did you enjoy the show? Burlesque is the premier attraction here, I'm afraid. Other than gambling, that is."

"It was fine," she said. "Very entertaining."

He started to say something, but before he could, one of the soldiers appeared and whispered into his ear. Dominic nodded and turned toward Claire.

"I'm afraid I must leave you for a short time," he said. "Lopez will escort you back to the hotel, where we'll be attending a party. I'll meet you there in a couple of hours."

He smiled and walked away. Lopez held out his arm and the two left the building. Outside, a handful of young men moved busily between the exiting patrons, each one handing out fliers, which advertised another more lascivious venue. Claire took one of the fliers and saw it featured a blurry, photocopied image of a fat woman blindfolded and bound. She looked at Lopez, who snatched the paper away and crumpled it. One of the young men stepped forward but withdrew when Lopez opened his jacket to show his gun.

"Let's go," said Lopez, as the limousine pulled forward, his voice low and mealy, as if he whispered through a metallic fan.

He opened the door and Claire stooped down to see the sneezy soldier waiting within. She adjusted her dress and slid inside. Someone shouted something to Lopez, who turned and withdrew his pistol. The crowd eyed him lazily, few showing any signs of interest, much less concern. After a few moments more, Lopez sat down within the vehicle and closed the door.

"Everything alright?" Claire asked.

Lopez gave an affirmative nod, as he slipped the gun back into its holster. The limo pulled out into the street and moved through the city streets, which had thinned out considerably since their arrival. Twenty minutes later, they pulled up to the hotel.

The moment she stepped out the limousine, a gray-haired doorman approached and asked her name.

"Claire Foley," she said.

Lopez exited the limo and reached into his jacket pocket, removing two one hundred-dollar bills that looked as bright and new as the day they were made.

"Escort her to the party," he said.

The old man nodded and saw her inside, where he passed her over to an elevator attendant. This was a tall, square looking man with thick eyebrows which had begun to meander. Without saying a word, he escorted her to the elevator and waited for the shimmering gold doors to slide apart.

"The party is on the roof," he said through his brambly beard.

"Do I have time to visit my room?" she asked, but he didn't answer.

They rode together, neither talking, the elevator soaring upward without the slightest hint, save for the gentle swimming in her stomach once it reached the top.

The second the elevator doors opened, anxiety flooded her chest. The rooftop was filled with wealthy, well-dressed men, escorted by exquisite-looking women who looked as if they'd been grown in a lab. Tall, buxom and beautiful, they all wore colorful party masks with fluffy feathers jutting up from one side. As she stepped out the elevator, a man approached and looked her over.

"I think this one," he said, and he presented a gold mask accented with a pretty little red feather.

Without speaking, she took the mask and put it on, feeling both ridiculous and relieved all in one moment. She left the man and approached the bar.

"Champaign or something stronger?" the young bartender said, as if sensing her unease.

"A martini," she said.

While she waited, she scanned her surroundings. Men huddled together and shook hands, while their dates stood quietly, their flawless little faces looking vapid and bored.

"Ever been to one of these things?" the bartender asked, as he served her drink.

"No."

"There's an orgy at the end."

She smiled at him, but he just turned and walked away.

"Ah, there you are," Dominic said, as he approached through the crowd. He wore a fresh tailored suit and as he approached, his cologne stung her eyes.

"I hope you haven't been waiting long," he said, as he took her hand.

"Just a few minutes."

"Please," he said, "let me introduce you to a handful of acquaintances. Some of these people are worth much in the way of amusement, I assure you."

They approached an old, fat man with a deep purple scar on the side of his neck and a sparse layer of thin gray hair strung horizontally across his freckled head. Claire felt her lip curling spontaneously at the sight of this creature, but the beautiful young girl clutching his arm seemed oblivious to any defects.

"Jean Paul," Dominic said loudly, as the old man grinned in delight. "Let me introduce you to my good friend Claire."

"Enchanted," Jean Paul said with a slight accent that was difficult to place. "What a lovely girl you are. Dominic is fortunate to have such a beauty for company this evening."

Claire accepted his outstretched hand, and he placed a moist kiss on top.

"Jean Paul is an investor, but that's not what makes him interesting," Dominic said. "He is also a particularly accomplished explorer, who's been to places most people have never seen."

Claire raised her eyebrows in a forced demonstration of interest.

"This is true," Jean Paul said. "I enjoy traveling very much and have met many astonishing people on my journeys."

Dominic looked at Claire and smiled.

"You see, Jean Paul has no interest in things that lure many travelers: history, architecture, culture and whatnot."

Claire nodded.

"What does attract you?" she asked.

"Why the cuisines, my dear," he said with a grin. "Or more specifically, the rich oddities which some cultures ingest for sustenance and ritual alike."

Claire pinched her eyebrows together.

"You see, Jean Paul has a unique appetite for things you and I might find repugnant," Dominic said. "Please, Jean Paul, share."

"Yes, Dominic is correct. I have eaten things you might consider odd; however, to the people who eat them on a regular basis, they are like your hamburgers and French fries." He took a sip of his drink and peered at her thoughtfully. "For example, in Europe, as you may know, they enjoy blood pudding, which is comprised largely of coagulated blood drawn from pigs, cattle, sheep or what have you: earthy, meaty like iron. In Asia, they have bat paste, where a live bat is forced into a vat of boiling milk until it becomes malleable enough to be mashed into an edible pulp. Elsewhere, balut, hasma, jellied moose nose, countless dishes consisting of fried or boiled rats, hornets, spiders, roaches and other arthropods."

Claire put a hand to her stomach.

"Ah, a common reaction, my dear," Jean Paul said. "However, had you tasted some of this, you would assuredly change your opinion. Some are quite tasty once you get past the textures. In fact, I've adopted many to my usual menu. Casu marzu, for instance, which is made when the rind of a whole Pecorino cheese is removed to give flies an opportunity to inject their larvae. As the maggots feed, the acid from their digestive tracts works to break down the fat in the cheese, leaving a particularly unique flavor. Currently, this cheese is banned by the European Union due to ridiculous health concerns, so it must be procured on the black market; however, it is a treat worth pursuing, I can assure you."

Claire looked at Dominic, who smiled with sincere amusement.

"Tell her what else you've added to your personal menu, Jean Paul."

A wry little grin shot across the old man's face.

"It's alright?" he asked Dominic, who nodded and put his hand out.

"Please."

Claire furrowed her brows as Jean Paul cleared his throat.

"Well, you see my dear, throughout my life, one of my largest curiosities has centered on the consumption of human beings, themselves, by other human beings. So, I made a point to explore regions of the world where this was said to still occur. More often than not, these turned out to be falsehoods; however, occasionally, I found success."

He squinted and licked his lips.

"The way it was prepared by natives left it stringy and tough and somewhat sour; but since then, I've found if you soak the meat in milk prior to consumption, the flavor is much better."

Claire moved a little closer to Dominic.

"You eat people?"

Jean Paul smiled.

"No one you know, my dear." The old man chuckled and put his arm around his date's slender waist. "Money brings privileges."

An awkward silence fell upon the circle before Dominic finally spoke.

"Well, we should mingle elsewhere," he said. "Jean Paul, as always, thank you for entertaining us."

Jean Paul nodded and held out his hand.

"It was a pleasure."

Claire placed a reluctant hand atop the old man's wrinkled fingers, and he pushed another warm, moist kiss against her knuckles.

"Nice to meet you," she said, and then they were off to meet other guests, who all seemed perfectly comfortable describing their own unique lifestyles and habits.

By the end of the night, Claire's mind was reeling.

"Have you not been entertained?" Dominic asked with a little smirk.

"It's certainly been something."

As if from thin air, Lopez approached and whispered something into Dominic's ear. He frowned and set his drink on a table.

"I'm sorry to say I must leave you again," he said, and then the two walked away.

Claire watched them weave through the crowd which had thinned considerably in the last hour; and then they both disappeared behind a big black door. She swallowed the last of her martini and returned to the bar.

"Where has everyone gone?" she asked the bartender.

"To the after-party in the suite below," he said. "The elevator attendant will take you there at your request."

She looked around at the sparse crowd and saw Jean Paul grinning at her from across the room.

"Maybe I'll have a look."

She ordered another drink and headed toward the elevator. The attendant asked her floor, and when she told him, his eyebrows lifted. Seconds later, the doors opened. He gave a gracious nod, and she stepped out into a beautifully decorated hallway that stretched out beneath dim lighting. Quickly, a very large security guard rushed forward and asked her intentions.

"I was told there was an after-party on this floor?"

"Yes," he said politely. "Just down the hallway and through those doors."

She nodded and proceeded the rest of the way, but as she approached the doors, something stopped her. It was noise, strange, muffled noise, the origin of which her mind could not resolve. She looked over her shoulder toward the security guard, but he only smiled and nodded.

Without responding, she turned back toward the doors and took hold of the knobs. With a sudden jerk, she pulled them open to reveal a mob of nude men and women engaged in an astounding array of fleshly acts. She froze in the doorway and watched as women engaged in oral obligations, while men took them from behind. Only inches away from them, men wrestled together, their bodies entangled in a twitching diversity of lurid homosexual acts. In one far corner, three men had their way with a woman who appeared to be drugged. A few feet from them, a very young girl lay unconscious, her makeup smeared, arms covered with human bite marks.

The center of the room was like one mass of skin, mouths, genitals and writhing legs. Men and women switched partners indiscriminately without regard for age or gender, each moving from body to body without making eye contact with its host. And all the while, some just sat in chairs watching it all, cigarettes dangling from their fingers, serious looks on their faces.

At last, Claire drew the eyes of some of the men and a few stood, their naked bodies glossy with sweat, faces hungry, like animals at the sight of unspoiled meat.

Without thinking, she fled down the hallway and slipped past the security guard who was busy reading a newspaper. He opened his mouth to speak, but before a single word dropped from his lips, she had successfully summoned the elevator and made her escape.

An hour later, she sat at the rooftop bar sipping a martini, while the bartender talked about this and that. She was beginning to think Dominic would not return at all, but just as she contemplated an escape, a man arrived with a message.

"Mr. Betancur wanted to me to apologize for leaving you unattended for so long and would like you to join him for a drink in his apartment suite three floors down."

Having delivered his message, the man turned abruptly and walked away.

Claire finished her drink and said goodbye to the bartender.

"Goodbye to you," he said with a smile that brought a unique appeal to his ordinary face.

"Can you tell me which apartment suite is Mr. Betancur's?" she asked.

"Three floors down," he said, as he wiped the bar.

"Yes, but which one?"

"No," he said. "He occupies the whole floor."

When she met the elevator attendant this time, he greeted her with a familiar smile.

"You, again?"

"Me, again."

"Mr. Betancur's floor?" he asked.

She nodded and he pressed the floor and crossed his hands.

When the doors opened, Lopez stood before her.

"This way," he said.

They crossed through a hallway, the walls pale, elegant paintings placed here and there. When they reached the end of the hall, they stood before a large steel door. Lopez approached a keypad to the right of it and tapped in a series of numerical codes, the buttons glowing green with every tap. When he finished, a soft click went off and the door popped open. Lopez took a large step back and turned his palm upward.

"Please," he said.

Claire nodded respectfully and entered, closing the door behind her.

Inside, it was all white leather and tasteful extravagance, a tiny fire burning within a massive fireplace, a candle in every direction.

"Have a seat," Dominic said from behind a little wet bar situated in the far corner.

She put her head down and crossed the room, his eyes tracing her every step, studying her as she smoothed the backside of her dress to sit. He finished whatever it was he'd been doing and approached her, a single glass of scotch in his hand. He looked as if he'd just come from the party, the belt gone from his black slacks, the tie from his white shirt, two or three buttons undone to reveal the upper portion of his chest. He sat beside her and leaned back, his knees spread open as if he'd known her long enough to expect anything and everything without asking.

"Would you like a drink?" he asked, as he sipped his scotch.

"Yes, thank you."

He lowered his eyebrows and swallowed, a shallow hiss escaping from his damp lips.

"Help yourself."

She smiled as if he were joking, but his demeanor remained unchanged. She lifted to her feet and made her way over to the bar. He watched her the way, noting the ticks of her high heels against the white tile.

She surveyed the liquors: everything you could imagine and some she'd never seen before. Without thinking much about it, she made a martini and splashed a pair of olives inside. She returned with her drink in hand, while he took in all her subtle movements through lazy eyes. In her absence, he had moved to the center of the couch, and his face flashed a cunning little smirk that made him look somewhat malevolent. She sat beside him and sipped her drink.

"You are very beautiful, do you know that?" he said, his words afflicted by drunkenness. "I find you very attractive."

He rested his arm over the couch behind her and leaned in closer, his fingers lightly touching the ends of her long hair.

"I've been thinking of this moment all night," he said, as he moved in for a kiss.

She lowered her head and turned away.

He moved back and dropped his eyebrows.

"Is there a problem?" he asked, as he withdrew a pack of cigarettes from his pocket.

She shook her head.

"It's nothing to do with you, Dominic, but I have no interest in a romantic relationship with anyone at the moment. As I said before, my only interest is to fulfill my duties and return to my life."

He held a very beautiful lighter up to his cigarette and lit it over a pulsing blue flame.

"Who said anything about romance?" he asked, as he exhaled a cloud of white smoke.

She eyed him carefully.

"I'm only looking for a bit of fun for the evening, nothing more."

She looked at her drink.

"Even still."

His face hardened and he stood up. She watched him cross to the other side of the room and take a seat in a chair.

"Let me tell you a story," he said. He paused to suck from his cigarette, his eyes lowered to the floor, eyebrows squinted as if he were deep in thought. He exhaled and scratched the dark whiskers which had grown noticeable this late in the evening. "Once, there was this girl, a dancer here in the city."

He drew from his cigarette once more, a bright orange kernel flaring and then fading. He took it away from his mouth and continued, while flittering streams of white smoke escaped his lips.

"She was a beautiful girl. Long blond hair, endless legs, a mouth that seemed to be always wet, always pink and wet."

He raised his cigarette and took another deep, long pull, his eyes studying her face, its beauty marred by fear despite her best efforts. He smiled as he inhaled, thin wisps of smoke escaping upward along the sides of his sucking cheeks. Finally, he took the cigarette from his lips and turned away.

"When she first came here, she was a clueless cunt, nothing more," he continued. "I took her in because these types arouse my interest." He turned his hand over toward her as if to make an example, his eyes drifting upward, as if he struggled to remember. He put the glass of scotch to his lips and took two large swallows. Then he wiped his mouth with his sleeve and placed the glass on the table beside him.

"She was like my pet for a while." He looked toward her, his eyes dark in the low, amber light, shadows hovering over them, making him seem inhuman, demonic.

"These types," he said, gesturing toward her again with a flip of the hand. "They are willing for anything, even if they think otherwise. Their lives before: gray to them, oppressive. When they come to me, they are like rutting animals, asses up in the air, their scent so obvious. I have them however I want them, and they go willingly, begging for me to degrade and humiliate them, loving it."

He smiled to himself, as he flicked ashes into a ceramic tray. Claire shifted in her seat, her eyes on the door, on anything in the room that might pass for a weapon.

"This girl I speak of, she was very kindhearted, but as I said, she had no clue. It took me no time to adopt her for my purposes, and soon she recognized her fate."

He shook his head and ashed in the ceramic tray once more, his back turned toward her, eyes scanning the room, appreciating his great wealth.

"Ultimately, I bored of her," he went on. "However, I decided to maintain ownership of her, so I instructed her as such and put her in a small apartment downtown, under guard of course."

He put his cigarette out in the tray and turned to face Claire.

"A time or two, she made attempts to free herself; however, these were met with brutal discipline that left her scarred and useless to any man save a pimp."

He lifted his eyebrows and offered an empathetic frown.

"Sadly, these events drove the girl to cut through her wrists with a large shard from a broken bathroom mirror."

His eyes drifted to the floor for a moment while he thought. Then they trickled upward and bored forth, the pupils seeming to swell according to his will.

"You see, she knew it was her only way out, and so she took it."

He shook his head slowly.

"There was simply no other way."

A harsh knocking slammed against the front door, and Claire jumped in her seat. Dominic smiled and stood, dusting his slacks and then making his way across the room. He called through the door, and Lopez gave an earnest response. Dominic opened the door and stepped into the hallway, closing Claire inside.

Immediately, she took to her feet and scampered to the kitchen. She opened drawers in search of knives, but she only found forks, spoons, butter knives and chopsticks. She slammed the drawers closed and ran down the hallway, checking door after door to find every one locked. Finally, she put her hand around a doorknob and gave it a successful turn. The door opened to reveal a closet packed with heavy coats and a stack of cardboard boxes.

She looked over her shoulder to make sure she was still alone, then she tore one of the boxes open and put a hand over her mouth. Inside, there were pictures of women, their lifeless bodies sprawled awkwardly upon cement floors, wrists tied together, knife wounds decorating their skin, their vacant eyes staring off into nowhere, mouths agape.

She heard the soft thwack of the front door unsealing and lost hold of the box, the photos flittering in the air and drifting in all directions. As the soles of his shoes clapped the tile entryway, she fell to her knees and grabbed the pictures in bunches, pushing them into the box and closing it shut.

She jumped to her feet, but the shifting weight inside the box threw it off balance, and it slipped through her hands and crashed to the floor. His footsteps grew louder, thumping the tile with a growing urgency, like big wooden hammers pounding a hollow drum.

In a panic, she bent over and gathered it all up, pushing it awkwardly into the closet and closing the door just as his tall, broad silhouette filled the space at the end of the hall.

"I need to use the bathroom," she said, her eyes darting softly between his shadowed face and the carpeted floor.

He approached her without speaking and took her arm with an unforgiving hand.

"This way," he said, as he led her back up the hallway and into the living room. He released her and pointed to a door in the far corner of the room. "Fix your makeup while you're in there."

She hurried to the bathroom and closed herself inside. She opened every drawer, but found only cotton swabs, linens and decorative soaps. She closed the last one and studied the mirror. A ragged, shaken woman looked back, her tears polluted with mascara, eyes bleeding ink. Soon she was sobbing, her hands on the countertop, body shaking.

A fist smashed against the door, and she flinched at its force.

"Don't take all night," he said from outside.

"I'll be right out," she said with a quivering voice not her own.

As his footsteps faded, she straightened her face until the girl in the mirror looked more like the one from a few hours before. Finally, she put her makeup bag back inside her purse and opened the bathroom door.

Outside, he sat on the couch with his back to her, a fresh cigarette dangling from his hand.

"Come join me," he said.

She moved slowly toward him, taking a seat on the other side of the couch.

"Now, now," he said, as he patted the space immediately next to him. "Slide closer."

She swallowed hard and slid over, his left arm engulfing her slight body. He smelled of cigarettes and too much cologne, and the stink of it nearly gagged her. He placed his hand over the top of her head and pressed her face against his chest.

He began massaging her scalp, and as he did, his fingers gathered up bunches of her hair and twisted it into a firm handle.

"Unbutton me," he whispered, as he exhaled a cloud of cigarette smoke.

"No," she said, turning her head away.

In a rage, he yanked her upward, nearly tearing the skin from her skull. She let out a shrill cry and tears welled in the corners of her eyes.

"You don't ever tell me no," he whispered into her ear. "Do you understand?"

When she didn't respond, he leaned in and took her earlobe between his teeth. She shrieked as he clamped down. He chewed the flesh until she thought she might pass out from the pain. Then he finally released and spit blood onto the lap of her dress.

"Do you understand now?" he whispered into her ear.

"Yes."

He re-gripped her hair and brought her closer.

"Wait," she said. "Please, just let me have a drink first. Just one drink."

He paused for a moment and then released her.

"Make it quick."

She got to her feet and turned to go, but before she'd made even a single step, he had her by the wrist.

"Get me one too."

He drank his glass empty and pushed it into her hand. She took it and made her way to the bar.

While he sat smoking, she looked about for knives without success. And then, from the corner of her eye, she saw something metal give off a glittering sparkle of refracted light. She turned to see a corkscrew sitting atop the marble counter.

She looked over to Dominic, but he was busy with his cigarette, his lips moving along with whatever stream of thought sifted through his drunken mind. Without hesitation, she took up the corkscrew and slipped it under her skirt, twining the coiled metal tip in the string of her underwear, where it crossed over the top of her left thigh. She filled his glass with scotch and returned to the couch.

She handed him the glass, and he took it without looking, a little wrinkled smirk on his face. With a measured haste, she sat next to him, pulling her skirt upward in bunches to hide the bulging corkscrew handle. He placed his cigarette in the ashtray and downed his entire drink in three large swallows.

Chills climbed her spine as she watched him drink, his throat bulging grotesquely as it consumed. When he'd drained the glass dry, he set it on the table and wiped the slick from his mouth. He turned and smiled, his bold eyes hungry and showing obvious signs of intoxication.

"Where were we?" he said, as he palmed the back of her head and gathered up a bunch of her hair once more.

He forced her down again, and this time she offered no resistance. But before he knew what was happening, she'd taken hold of him with all her strength, her fingers rooting in around his vulnerability, her grip like a vice.

Wails of agony escaped his throat as she clamped down harder. He released her hair and pried against her hand, but as he lunged forward, she withdrew the corkscrew with her other hand and plunged it into the side of his neck.

The shiny metal sunk into the fleshy tissue, a string of dark purple blood bowing upward and splashing against the white tile floor.

He put both hands to his throat to stop up the bleeding, but it boiled out between his fingers as he gurgled up words. Claire scrambled to her feet and froze, the corkscrew still dangling from her hand, the coils congested with gore. Dominic staggered to his feet and stumbled toward her, his eyes flaring wildly, face painted with a medley of fear, blood and rage.

He came at her full bore and put his fingers around her neck, but the moment his hands left the wound, a red waterfall escaped, and he dropped to the ground, his handsome face pallid, eyes uninhabited.

Claire looked down at his lifeless body, half expecting him to spring back up to his feet. She kicked at him, the toe of her high heel shoe digging into his ribs without conjuring any sort of response. Once convinced, she turned her attention toward the door, approaching it cautiously, her body trembling and heaving with great exasperated breaths.

In the corner, a security monitor showed the goings on in the exterior hallway lobby. She watched Lopez pacing around outside, his hand in his pocket, a drowsy look on his face. Without hesitation, she worked the locks on the door and opened it. Lopez turned abruptly, his body straightening to prepare for the sight of his boss. But instead, he saw only Claire, her dress and skin saturated in blood.

"Please," she said, her eyes welling up with tears. "There's been an accident."

Lopez hurried forward and looked inside the apartment, his face paling at the sight of Dominic Betancur. He reached into his jacket, but before he could grasp the butt of the gun, Claire drove the corkscrew into the back of his neck.

This time, her aim was exact, and Lopez collapsed to the ground as if his soul had been plucked free. She stood over him for several seconds, the corkscrew handle sticking out the back of his spine, as if it powered an enormous wind-up toy. She removed her shoes and scampered to the elevator. She pressed the button and waited, her heart thumping wildly as if it wanted out. Within seconds the door opened, and the bearded elevator operator greeted her with a look of great worry.

"Please," she said, her palms turned upward. "Mr. Betancur needs your help."

Without thinking, the man fled the elevator and sprinted for the apartment. As he did, Claire took his place and furiously tapped the ground floor button. As if beckoned by some noiseless tone, the operator stopped and turned.

"Hey!" he bellowed, the depth of his voice rugged and frightening. "What are you doing?"

Claire frantically pressed the button several times more, as the thud of his boot heels grew louder and louder.

"Get out of there!"

At last, the doors flashed out of their hiding places and raced toward one another; but before they met, the burly operator thrust his hand between. The doors met his arm and relented, the entryway opening enough for him to squeeze between, his big body swelling before her, eyes red with rage.

A rush of fear washed over her, as the furious man moved forward and took her by the arms, his massive hands enveloping them whole, so his fingers touched on the other side. Without thinking, she let out a soft little cry and brought her knee upward in a sharp forward angle. The hard, bony kneecap struck true enough to draw a slobbering yowl that filled the elevator and hurt her ears.

As if all the oxygen had vanished, the operator collapsed onto the ground and clutched at his genitals, his face contorted, tears welling in the corners of his eyes. The elevator doors flared out again, this time stopping around the man's legs and withdrawing once more. In a panic, Claire stomped her heel into his shins, until he finally pulled them toward his chest and made room for the doors.

Immediately, she pressed the button to summon the doors back again, but they remained withdrawn, while the operator crawled to his knees.

"You fucking bitch," he gasped. "I'll kill you!"

Finally, the doors appeared again, and when the operator saw this, he staggered to his feet and limped forward, one hand stretched out, fingers clutching the air.

Claire held her hands to her mouth as the man encroached, his image growing slender between the closing elevator doors. Convinced he would interrupt them once more, she positioned herself to offer whatever defense she could muster, but just before his hand could slip between, the elevator sealed itself shut and began its descent.

As she drew closer to the lobby floor, she looked at her dress, which now resembled a costume from a horror film. When the elevator opened, a well-dressed old couple stood before her, their jaws agape at such an unexpected vision. She stepped between them and into the lobby, where gasps spread from person to person like a virus.

Through the hush, Romero rushed forward and took her by the arm.

"You're not going anywhere," he said, as he held his hand to an earpiece that barked instructions in low tones.

"Help me!" Claire yelled to the people in the lobby, but all seemed too shocked to move. "Please, help me, for God's sake!"

Finally, a large man in a cowboy hat stepped forward and blocked Romero's path.

"Hold it right there," he said. "Where are you taking this woman?"

Romero looked the man over.

"This is none of your concern. I advise you to stand aside."

A fire took life in the large man's eyes, and he cocked his hat back and pointed a thick finger at Romero.

"You're not taking her anywhere until we figure out what in the hell's going on."

A crowd started to form around the three, and this seemed to make Romero nervous. He looked from side-to-side and then released Claire's arm. The large man held out a hand, but before she could take it, Romero drove his empty palm into the front of the man's neck, knocking his hat backward and choking the breath from his throat.

The crowd gave a collective gasp, as the large man fell to his knees. Without hesitation, Claire turned and made a run for the exit, but just before she could grab the door handle, Romero had her arm again."

"You're not going anywhere," he whispered into her ear. "You'll pay for what you've done."

With that, he turned to face the lobby, but before he could focus his eyes, a large fist collided with his nose, and a crunching noise racketed across the room. Instantly, Romero lost consciousness and fell forward, his face landing hard against the floor.

Tooth fragments shot out and skipped across the tile, settling just in front of the old couple from the elevator, their faces advertising horror and disgust. The large man hovered over his fallen adversary, his left hand still clutching his throat, whistling, wheezing breaths passing between his purple lips.

"Are you alright?" a woman asked.

"I'm fine," he whispered. "Someone call the authorities."

As people gathered around him, he looked for the girl.

"Where's that woman?" he said to no one in particular.

Everyone looked around, but no one had an answer, and no one knew what to say, when the authorities finally arrived.

Made in United States
Cleveland, OH
24 June 2025